Sarah Elliot was born in Newcastle and raised in Northumberland. She was diagnosed with dyslexia at the age of ten and turned to writing her own stories as a way of keeping up her skills. She has never looked back since.

She graduated from Swansea University in 2009 with a Masters in Creative and Media Writing and has had three plays performed by a theatrical group in Swansea. She currently works as an administrator in a care home in Newcastle and spends her free time socialising with friends, writing, and taking Petal, the Rottweiler, for long walks.

VOLF: SILVER

Amethyst Trilogy Book 1

Sarah Elliot

Volf: Silver

Amethyst Trilogy Book 1

To Alison and Mike
Aroo!! lets find the Volf and
well dec on the book. Darylcici
rules

SElliot

Vanguard Press

*Vanguard Press is an imprint of
Pegasus Elliot MacKenzie Publishers Ltd.*
www.pegasuspublishers.com

First published in 2016

Vanguard Press
Sheraton House Castle Park
Cambridge England

Printed and bound in Great Britain

To my Parents Lynn and Kevin for being supportive and constantly there for me when times have been hard.

To my friends Sam and Kirsty for bugging me to send off my stories and getting proved right.

Chapter 1

New Moon

The woods echoed with an un-natural silence that was only occasionally broken by the heavy sounds of bark ripping away from the trees; Ekata was only so glad that the snow was thick and heavy on the ground, as it made movement more cumbersome but it also made tracking the runaway Volf so much easier. Not that such a thing was of that much importance when running from two of the world's most deadly vampires, but the dark-haired girl would have given anything at that moment in time to be in the mountains further north. Those vast peaks she knew all too well, with their dark caves and hiding places and it was easy to out-run even the most cunning of eyes in all of those shadows but here in this heavy wood there was no point in wishing for anything.

Except, said a small voice somewhere deep in the back of her mind, that just maybe *he* would be here.

Letting out a half-strangled squeak of surprise as the ground in front of her gave way, Ekata tumbled down the side of a natural river bed and sloshed into the water. The water froze the air in her lungs and for a moment or two she felt nothing but panic and despair as her nose, eyes and ears were covered by the constantly tumbling water. Suddenly a hand latched onto her forearm and hauled her out, pulling her into the bank and throwing her into a thick clump of bramble. "Stay low and don't make a sound," a softly-spoken masculine voice spoke though Ekata could barely see any details as the water was still trickling into her eyes.

Some inner instinct made her listen to the voice and press into the side of the bank, remaining still and not moving. Though she became aware that the person whom owned the voice moved away from her but Ekata only lightly flicked an ear when she heard a branch snap.

"Siren," another voice whispered, the winds carrying it to her sensitive ears but this one the Volf knew all too well. "Be wary, we are far too close to their land now and if we enter it—"

"The wolves will make an impressive collection for Mother." The second voice was closer, smaller in power but lined with more than enough venom to suggest someone who belonged beyond the edge of insanity. Ekata knew all too well the deranged girl behind the voice, with her fiery red hair and dazzling hazel eyes but knew better than to betray her presence. Siren Du Winter may have been unhinged from reality most of the time, but was counted as one of the vampires' greatest assassins. However, the fear of her elder sister was not the reason that she remained completely still and trying desperately not to breathe.

No, the Volf remained exactly where she was because of the man with Siren. Possibly the only man she would ever truly be afraid of in the entire world. The soulless eyes were seeking for the slightest telltale sign of movement from atop the opposite side of the riverbank, pale grey pools that seemed almost too un-natural for the handsome face and long dark flowing hair that was just tinged with blue when the moonlight fell on it. Mephistopheles had been named after the devil's right-hand man of *Faust* fame and justified his inherited title perfectly. No one wanted to cross paths with him, not even herself and at one time, she had called him brother but by a different name.

Ekata chanced a flick of her amber eyes up towards the pair on the opposite river bank and thought for a moment that she saw a flicker of something different in the strange eyes of Mephistopheles but brushed it off as being nothing more than a reflection of light off the water. The elder vampire snorted and turned away, cape billowing around him. "Sneaky little half-breed, must've given us the slip. Downstream should be her direction."

There was a hiss and a rock landed in the water not two feet from where the Volf remained pressed against the welcoming mud, clearly Siren wasn't best pleased at the situation. "When I get my hands on that scrawny little neck..." She paused, almost thoughtfully, before sniffing the air. "How about a meal, dear brother? There is a fresh one just lying there waiting to be taken."

A frown rippled across the brow of the male and Ekata's white ears flicked curiously to the side. Footsteps moved to the edge of the riverbank, clearly the elder vampire was looking to see what the slightly mad one had spotted before spitting in disgust. "A mangy heap like that? It's nothing but skin and bones. If you want to feast on werewolf, my dearest Siren, I suggest you capture that one that was on patrol. Leave your hunger for now; we have bigger fish to catch."

Whatever arguments the girl had been going to give disappeared into the silence of the wood just as a fresh snow began to fall. Slowly the darkness gave way on its choking hold and let nature come back to life. An owl hooted distantly, the foxes and badgers began emerging from their dens to begin the nightly raid for food and even the small river began to lap lazily over the stones whereas before it had slunk silently around them. Pulling herself away from the bank, the Volf stole a glance up at the night sky and sniffed deeply for a few seconds. Both of her half-siblings were heading downstream and this was the perfect opportunity to escape.

Letting out a breath, which may have been a sigh of relief or trepidation, Ekata turned to head upstream to at least try and put as much distance between herself and those that hunted her. Though she found herself stopping short before she had even taken a step. There on the opposite bank, lay a young man, possibly only a few years older than herself with a dark tan to his skin and chocolate-coloured hair that was messily sprayed about on his head. His shirt was caught on some higher branches, exposing a long thin white scar which ran in a loop from his left shoulder to his right hip. A cut was evident on his forehead, presumably from when he had fallen down. Some inner instinct made her draw closer to the figure and despite the freezing cold water that only just started to brush away the dirt which clung to the age-old clothes, the Volf knelt down next to the boy and lifted his head out of the water.

A slight spluttering was her reward and a small smile graced her lips. "What are you doing out here all alone?" she asked, unaware that her pale fingers had wandered gently into the thick hair until an inner growl of her stomach made her look down. The small cut was actually much larger than she had originally thought; it was more like a huge graze to the back of his head as if someone had purposefully smashed into him. What was worse was that now her fingers were covered in running rivers of this unknown boy's blood and the side of her that frequently fought to gain dominance reared fully in force.

Before she really understood what was going on, she had dragged her tongue over her hand to savour the warm taste of the precious life fluid. Almost immediately a dreadful cough was ripped from her throat, followed by a burning sensation which ran in hot riveters up and down her spine. Both of her natural given genes fighting to repel the other even though such a thing was impossible to do.

The vampire craved blood; it needed to feed until the point of collapse. It wanted so badly to break free and tear this offering to pieces, drink its heart's content and then curl up for a long deep sleep away from the perishable light that the hours would eventually have to bring. Yet the blood stung and tore, ripped and destroyed, laced with natural poisons to make it undrinkable, a passage between two races that should never be crossed no matter what the situation.

The werewolf sought to survive, sought to strike out at the vampire and delve deeper into the wood to find a place to rest and heal. It didn't need the blood to survive; it wanted food, fresh raw meat with plenty of fat. The thrill of the hunt but it couldn't deny that since the sky was devoid of the moon, the power wasn't there.

For the Volf, being caught between the two worlds on a daily basis was one of the hardest things to do. Belonging to one side in an ageless and never-ending war was always a good starting point in life but what was one to do when they were neither one nor the other and yet both at the same time? Ekata Monet was one of a pair of twins that were half-vampire, half-werewolf, the illegitimate children of Cresta Du Winter, Vampire Lady of the North and some half-forgotten werewolf lover who had given her comfort when her husband passed away.

It was a fight to win out against the need to feed upon the boy's blood, but strangely a stirring from the fallen figure below made her stop and look down questioningly. "Don't." A voice, the same voice that had commanded her so easily before though now more ragged and rather hollow-sounding, drifted to her ears which twitched back and forth dislodging the clumps of dark hair which usually tried to cover them. "Please, my lady... my blood is not going to help you... at least not yet."

Ekata blinked slowly, trying to work out if this voice truly belonged to the boy currently resting on her lap or if it was a mere whisper inside her head. "I am no one's lady," she replied gently, leaning down just a little closer. "Why do you call me such things?"

Before an answer could be delivered, the faintest of faint crunches cut through the not-so-present silence and Ekata turned sharply. Her eyes detected nothing immediately wrong with the place that she was looking at, she was still within the forest that was old and grey, smelling of the deep sleep that winter brought upon all of the natural world but also of the presence of a werewolf pack. The bows of the trees were thick and ancient, protecting a few slow-growing saplings and the shrubbery was patchy, clinging to the trees as if they were some form of protection against the things that could live despite the weather.

There were shadows, but they were natural and did not appear that threatening. Gently she sniffed the air, twisting her head to look directly down the flow of the stream and still saw no signs of anything other than the normal woodland creatures. Her two vile elder half-siblings were still close by but were gradually heading further away from her location. However, their progress was slow, clearly they had sensed some change in the forest that was making them cautious. Werewolves were known to kill vampires who strayed onto their lands, regardless of allegiances, but normally there were very clear markers and Ekata did not recall seeing any as she fled from the enraged pair.

There was another sound, quite distinctly a paw being placed softly on some dried out leaves that had somehow managed to not be covered in snow and a shiver ran through her. The wolves were here, intent to see what had disturbed their lands and take care of it in the only way that they knew how. Without realising it, the will-o-wisp thin girl gently picked up the boy from the edge of the river and placed him so that he lay in a safer position. Her amber-coloured eyes never left the surrounding area however, constantly scanning for the first signs of danger, which could potentially spell her doom. "I have to go now, I am sure they will take pity on you," she spoke to the boy and turned to leave him where he was.

Suddenly there was a grip on her wrist, firm and gentle but strong. Turning back to the boy, Ekata paled slightly as he twisted his head directly towards her and began to open his eyes. "Stay... stay here. They will protect you...heal you...guide you." His voice sounded still highly rough but there was genuine concern in there, which scared the Volf more than the thought of some stranger tracking her down and potentially killing her. "I need you here, my lady... don't go, or else they'll catch you."

His eyes seemed to almost blaze with a dazzling silver light and they frightened her for reasons that she could not even begin to comprehend but there was also a certain draw in them as well. Without any call, despite the water which was now numbing her shoeless feet and the terrible beating of her heart, Ekata stepped closer to the boy who simply tilted his head back in response. He was still not one hundred per cent there, that she was sure of because no one would ever be able to look upon her and call her a lady in this digesting and disheveled state, but something buried deep within her knew exactly what to do. Her fingers gently cupped the sides of his face and her lips brushed deeply against his.

The air suddenly felt warmer and lighter somehow and unknown to the pair a circle had formed, roughly three foot in diameter and reminiscent of the early spring dawns. The snow temporarily disappeared from view, the water sloshing by glistening a faint blue and the old felled winter wood sprouting forth glorious green foliage that wrapped around the roots and then sprang forth with a white flower that looked very much like that of a dove whilst its five petals fanned out in perfect balance.

The wolf who had initially gone out to chase down his wayward cousin Fiero, stared in shock at the unfolding scene without any real understanding and for a second or two he forgot that he was supposed to keep himself low and quiet.

But Jared felt an inexplicable pull towards the scene and stepped forward boldly and with clear noise indicating his presence.

Ekata heard the approach of the wolf and pulled herself up. "I have to go," she whispered, turning quickly and running following the course of the stream. The Volf was quick to move, sloshing through the water and trying to find a way back up the side of the bank but Jared was far quicker and knew the lands all too well.

Leaping down, Jared paused for only a fraction of a second to check that his younger cousin was still alive and breathing for now before taking off swiftly after the strange girl in his wolf form. His white fur shimmered in the rays of sunlight from the small path of spring which surrounded Fiero still. He had no time to admire it as he knew he could not allow this girl to ge away.

The ground was raw and hard against her bare feet but despite the pain, the girl kept on running. Spotting a low-hanging branch, she made a grab and hoisted herself up, back onto the relatively dry land where the going would be slightly easier. However, unbeknownst to the Volf, she had just entered the marshes, with their long, spidery vines crisscrossing the ground and the moss grew thick and heavy, even in the middle of a horrendous winter.

Ekata didn't even make it fifteen paces into the dangerous marsh before her already bruised and cut feet snagged on one of the lines and sent her tumbling straight into the thick, boggy water. It rushed straight up her nose and mouth, causing desperate thrashing from the girl as the shock of the ice-cold water sent stabs of utter panic and muscle spasms throughout her body. Something strong was pulling her down into the dark water, though whether more of the vines or something far more ancient that lurked under the surface she could not tell and a desperate need to get out of this watery grave engulfed her. Kicking out, the Volf finally found something solid, possibly a rock or just some sunken tree and made a dash for the surface.

Ice had somehow formed over the top, thick and heavy, able to withstand her desperate hands smashing against it, even with the odd silver glow that came from the tips of her fingers. She didn't want to die like this, couldn't die like this, there was still so much for her to do in the world, so much that she had to mend and fix. The palm of her hand found itself suddenly stuck to the thickening ice just as her senses began to fade, the water gleefully about to claim its next victim. The next second however there was a sudden harsh intake of air into her lungs and the water was gone.

"Cough it up," a voice was saying, different from the one before, and strong arms were hauling her half-frozen body away from the surface. "Get it out of you! Old Man river, release her! You don't get to claim this one!"

Hardly able to think straight, Ekata did what only came naturally to her at this point and coughed up as much of the vile-tasting water as she could do. She was barely aware of the words the werewolf was saying to her, only just about able to digest the fact that he had saved her despite being the one who had been chasing her before. Twisting around to look up at him, whilst still desperately trying to take a breath that didn't slash her throat into a million pieces, she stared up at the wolf who in human form appeared to be somewhere in his late twenties with a white and grey turn to his hair and green eyes. He did not resemble the boy she had talked to on the bank at all. Breathing heavily, she coughed harshly a few times before eventually managing to stumble out, "Why?"

The wolf glared directly ahead of himself, poised as if he was ready for battle. "Because of them."

Ekata twisted her head to the side, fighting off another wave of nausea and disorientation before she blinked in terror. Siren and Mephistopheles were standing on the edge of the marsh, looking just about ready to kill the pair of them. Jared just grinned. "They can't take another step... the vampire defenses are just in front of them. They'll be dead meat if they even put so much as a pinky toe into it."

The almost childish glee in the boy's voice vanished as the girl in his arms suddenly turned with a violent, gut-wrenching cough and blood splattered onto the roots of the snow-strewed tree.

Without pausing to think of what he was doing or the consequences of his actions, Jared grabbed the girl and hauled her into his large strong arms. He set off towards the Den, knowing that his mother would be the best person to deal with the poison coursing through the strange girl's veins.

He didn't fail to spot the silver swirls which began to glow on her skin; however, that just made him run all the more faster to reach the safety of home.

Chapter 2

Bandages

"Father, you have got to listen to me on this one!" Jared virtually cried, trying his best not to leap at the older wolf who was currently staring at the wall blankly after being told about the two who had been brought in. It wasn't so much that he was ignoring Jared, Rosario knew his wayward son well enough to know that he did not sprout fairy stories and lies but it was just very hard to believe. "I mean, go to the river bank and you'll see the flowers. They didn't disappear in the slightest," the younger continued, hoping that he wasn't being considered a liar by the alpha.

Rosario turned his pale blue eyes on his son, blinking gently in an effort to focus without having to resort to his glasses that hung around his neck. "It's not that I don't believe you, it's just that it is a hard thing to believe... plus I never dreamt that she would end up here with me after all that happened."

Jared couldn't help but flick his ears in confusion at the statement but before he could ask, Rosario seemed to realise what he had said and quickly shook his head before standing up and beginning to head down the corridor towards the guest bedroom. "Don't worry about it, just something from my past that I hoped would not come back to haunt me. You say she was being chased by two vampires?"

Sobering up a little, Jared nodded whilst regarding his father with an expert eye. Whilst on the surface the other looked surprisingly well kept for his age, the signs of wear and tear were beginning to show. There were patches of skin that were stained with liver spots too big to be completely natural and age-old winding scars that racked across his arms and chest though today these were covered over by a plain-looking shirt. There were wrinkles forming on the old face, more than he had ever dared to comment on but there was still a spark of life within the eyes though right at this moment in time, they looked more dulled than ever. A clear sign that something was bothering the old werewolf greatly which set alarm bells ringing in the younger man's head. "Yeah, a male and female. Unfortunately, they aren't your usual run-of-the-mill kind either, didn't take a single step into the marshes and avoided the repellents like the plague. Didn't even think of attempting to cross them in the slightest."

"Elders possibly?" Rosario asked with some strained hope in his voice, which was quickly dashed when the cub shook his head in response.

"I don't know but one was called Siren, that much I heard," Jared said softly, looking up to his father.

Rosario paled immediately, turning his full attention onto the girl who was now lying on the bed in the guest room and took a harder look towards her. If this was indeed the child, he thought it was then by all that was holy and unholy they were going to be in a whole heap of new trouble. Though there was a part of him that was secretly overjoyed to see the girl back, even looking as though she had literally gone through hell granted but alive and as she should be.

"Never mind about those vampires." Stefina's voice cut into the conversation, leaning just on the doorframe to the room where the girl was currently being kept. "I want to know what she was doing out there all alone, half-starved to death and why in Nix's name Fiero went out in this accursed weather."

Casting his eyes over to his lovely little wife, Rosario couldn't help but feel just a bit proud of her natural mothering instincts towards the pair of them. He was more than used to hearing her worry over Fiero, his nephew had proven to be a spirited little thing from the second he had recovered from the horrific slaying of his family and Stefina always had a soft spot for the unruly cub. But to hear her going on about the strange girl as if she were just a distant pack member was a relief. Not that he had doubted it for one second of course, Stefina took virtually any man, woman, child, vampire, werewolf or changer in without a complaint and would care for them like they were her own flesh and blood. Of course if anyone crossed her then hell hath no fury.

Gently he smiled at her and shook his head. "Until she wakes up I only have a few weak guesses. Can I take a look at her?"

"No." Stefina's voice was strict and straight to the point. "I've got several herbal remedies on the go and the last time I let you anywhere near them you ended up giggling on the floor like a new born cub for two days."

Trying to hide his laughter, Jared bit his lip before sobering up as his mother's glare fell on him in deep scrutiny. "Can we talk to Fiero then? I get the impression that he's awake or at least on some form of consciousness that does not equate to sleep."

Stefina sighed, glaring at her son in a playful manner. "You're starting to sound too much like that old uncle of yours, Jared Fernell. Yes, you can see him for a little while because I need to brew up a burdock tea to sort the fool out. You see that you give him a firm telling-off though, Rosario, and get him to tell you what he was doing running off in the middle of the night and worrying his aunty half to death." To emphasize the point, Stefina poked her long-established mate in the chest with a metal spoon which always stuck out of one of her many apron pockets.

Grinning, the alpha wolf nodded and watched as the bustling mother headed down towards the kitchen and cellars. "A right chip off the old block is your mother, couldn't find another like her in a hundred years of searching."

"Thank the nymphs for that," Jared said cheekily, heading towards Fiero's room. "I don't think the world could take it." Of course, he was joking because there was no way he would ever be nasty about his mother other than in jest. Stefina was a godsend amongst werewolf mothers and he considered himself extremely lucky to have her as his own good old mum. "Wish Fiero wouldn't act so much like her at times though, it gets really freaky when he does."

Whilst only a few years younger than Jared, Fiero had always appeared to be mature beyond his years and was at that stage in life where the choices began to seriously matter.

Should he stay with the pack and become a hunter or would it be wiser for him to head out into the world to find his own place amongst the ever-changing circumstances that were governed by it all. Rosario had no illusions that the cub would stay with them, ever since he could virtually walk the little scamp had been frequently found way outside of the boundaries or straying into other packs' territory with little more than a 'how do you do' to the resident wolves. The old wolf had lost track of the amount of times he had received either an exhausted messenger or more recently a very annoyed-sounding phone call, one of the few modern accessories to the human world that the wolves agreed to bring into their dens, telling him to come and collect Fiero.

The only problem was that most of the time the boy would have some explanation for why he had gone outside of the boundaries so punishment was hard but of late he had stopped going on his random outings. If anything, Rosario got the distinct impression that the boy was waiting for something to happen or for someone to arrive. He had taken plenty of sentry watches and had scored the parameter of the land far more times than was really necessary but the old wolf had presumed that it was just simply the boy growing up and thought nothing more of it.

Now the appearance of a girl whom he had once been a guardian to thought lost to the wilds and the fact that his nephew had gone out into the woods in the middle of the night when he had no reason to do so, Rosario couldn't help but begin to have some very strange thoughts. The type that he normally didn't like to have either as they involved a man whom he trusted to the ends of the earth but hadn't talked to in fifteen years. Someone was bound to be informing

Alcarde of what was going on but Rosario did not know if that was a good idea or not.

Upon reaching the room, which Fiero inhabited, both father and son hesitated at the doorway and listened. A soft voice, clearly Fiero's but spoken in low tones, was coming from inside the room but the words were difficult to decipher and Rosario tilted his head a little to the side in order to increase his hearing range.

Grabbing a notepad and pen, which had been left on one of the many tables outside of the room, Rosario quickly scribbled down what was being said, hoping that he did not miss a single word out. Though very quickly he found himself recognising the verse and felt a shiver go through his spine.

"Et a flumine per astra ,
Invicem , et inveniet
Spes mea es amica mea,
Per omnia saecula saeculorum ,
Tempestivus a prima a sole
Ad cor fovendum
Signa fate
Converte nos in unum
Pacem et concordiam,
Ut nostra fiat aut ortus
Sed ex parte stabo
Per omnia saecula saeculorum
Tu es domina
Qui immutare non possunt
Sustinui te reverti
Ita , quod mundus sit
Ut sit"

"Father," hissed Jared, not wanting to disturb the older wolf but feeling slightly annoyed at the lack of response from the other. "What is he doing?"

"Talking in an old Latin script," Rosario said without thinking, for the second time that day. "Appears to be reciting the poem of Aquilegia."

Jared stared up at his father, knowing that he should not pry into such things as he had been forbidden to ask about anything to do with the Hunters from that day that Fiero had been brought into their care, but too intrigued to let his questions go unanswered. "What's that got to do with anything that's going on?" A tactful question that covered many different angles without giving anything obvious away, or so the younger wolf thought.

Rosario paused, listening to the verse quietly before saying, "It is supposed to be a message written by the Silver Knight to the Silver Maiden so that when they are eventually rejoined in mortality they will be able to know one another." Slowly realization dawned on the alpha wolf and deliberately he pushed open the door to the boy's room in order to avoid any more questions. He was definitely getting far too involved in this whole scenario and he didn't want to think where it would all lead to.

Fiero looked up as the two males entered the room and quickly looked down and away as if he were hiding something. There was a smell of guilt about him but it was overpowered by curiosity and a desire to be somewhere else. A slight restless air was about his shoulders, the big toe on his right foot tapping constantly to some unheard rhythm and the haunch of his shoulders displaying all too well that right now he didn't want to be here in the slightest. Jared had only seen his younger cousin like this once and it was when he had first arrived at the den, looking somewhere between terrified of being alive and being in this strange place but there was something completely different about this situation, but it was impossible to put a paw on the specifics.

"I don't know," was the first words out of the cub's mouth before anyone got a chance to ask a question. "Something woke me last night and I was compelled to go out into the woods. It made no sense to me and I was the one who headed out there."

Jared blinked up at his father. "Has he got concussion?"

"From a fall like the one he had, more so than likely," Rosario said with a gentle sigh, staring at the sway of bandages that were wrapped around the young man's head, so reminiscent of his late mother that the old wolf had to take a moment to remind himself that he was not dealing with her. "What awoke you last night, Fiero?"

There was a pause before the boy shook his head. "I can't remember... it's like a hazy dream. I just remember the snow, ice and grabbing hold of someone, a girl I think and I turned to get something to try and warm her up 'cause she was as cold as the ice and then something hit me or I fell I don't know and then... then spring had come. Such a glorious spring, with real warmth and..." Trailing off Fiero opted not to talk about the next part of the dream. He knew it was wrong to not give full explanations to two of the men he could probably trust in the entire world but he didn't want to share *her* with them.

Lightly a sigh escaped his lips, recalling so vividly the image which had dominated his dreams for the past three months but never in such high-quality detail. He had presumed, at first that the girl in the silver-white dress with the black hair and strange eyes was one of those dream angels that visited for one purpose only but nothing like that had ever occurred in those dreams. Most of the time she had just been sitting by a riverbank, looking lost and forlorn but he could not bring himself to be any nearer to her as there were others present.

However, over the last week, he had noticed that the girl in the dreams had been closer to his hiding spot, dipping her feet into the crystal clear water or tending to the blossoming flowers and once sitting so close that when he reached out to touch her his fingers brushed gently over the fine, almost hidden white ears that were like silk under his touch. And then last night he had received a silent summon to head out into the woods and was convinced that she had been there.

She had kissed him, he remembered that much but for some insane reason he had not been able to focus on her properly. It was then he remembered the bang to the head as he had tumbled down and sighed. "I know it makes no sense but that's what happened. Honestly."

"I believe you, Fiero," Rosario said, kneeling down next to the cub. "Jared reported the same information to me and your aunt when he came back last night carrying the girl from the stream."

Sudden anger welled up in the young wolf and he glared at his brown-haired cousin, sending out an uncharacteristic growl which caused the white-haired elder to move instinctively backwards and away. The very idea that someone, especially another wolf, had clapped eyes on the angel from his dream just drove him to anger and a dreadful desire to protect. It only lasted an instant though before confusion strove across his face and he glanced at his uncle, hoping for some explanation as to what was going on.

However, Rosario had none, or at least one he wasn't prepared to give out right now. Instead he stared intently at the boy, before tilting his head backwards so that the natural light of the late sunrise glistened off the watery orbs. They shone a delicate silver, not striking as of yet from the normal grey-blue that they usually were but most distinctly the colour which should have brought pain to the werewolf. However, Fiero showed no outward signs of pain in the slightest.

That meant there was only one conclusion Rosario could draw, one that he was almost hoping wouldn't come entirely true. Gently he sighed. "I need to talk to Disreli about this."

"Why?" Fiero asked, panicking just a little bit at the mention of the elder wolf and his senior uncle. "What's wrong with me?"

Rosario gently shook his head. "Nothing that can't be easily remedied. I just want to confirm a few things before jumping to conclusions is all. You rest up, Fiero – you're going to need your strength over the next few days."

Chapter 3

Whispers

Brushing back the unkempt mess of hair from the boy's sweat-covered forehead, Disreli frowned before tutting loudly. Normally the smallest of small touches would be enough to wake the lightly sleeping Fiero, as he had never really gotten over that horrible night some seventeen years ago when fire had claimed his birth family, but it seemed right now that the cub was most definitely out for the count. "I will not try to see those eyes of his but I fear that you are correct in your assumptions, little Rosario. Though I guessed something was up on the day he arrived at our doorstep, half-dead and so lonely in a world filled with love." The ancient werewolf settled back a little on the bed in order to twist his so faint blue eyes onto his youngest brother with a faint smile. "Yet sometimes that is how the greatest amongst us start."

Rosario blinked. "If you suspected something you should have said, I would have taken him to the Hunters for protection and guidance." It was customary to be respectful towards one's elders but the pair had always had a strange relationship. They loved one another dearly, despite the huge age difference, were always the first to defend the other's actions or to offer assistance at a time of need. There was only one thing that they had disagreed on in their entire lives and it revolved around the day that Rosario joined the Hunters. Disreli had not been against the youngest son of his father joining, he just didn't want the then young, rebellious cub to be in a position of danger and Rosario being the then determined terror that he was back then, had insisted upon taking the most dangerous missions instead of remaining in the library and being an extremely useful researcher, just to prove the point that he was the best in all areas.

Shaking his head, the white strands far outweighing the grey of age now, the elder wolf sighed. "If I had he would have just become another dim-witted fighter with no real understanding of how the world works." A sly grin crossed Disreli's features. "Plus he who should not be named in my little brother's presence told me the best place for the boy would be here."

Immediately a flash of distrust shot through Rosario's eyes. "Why?"

"Something to do with the boy's father, I'm led to believe." A slight hunch of the shoulders came forth from Disreli but it was impossible to tell if it were a simple shrug or a shifting of body mass. "But even I was kept in the dark about what he knew. Don't count yourself as the only one who lost his faith in that man. It was a dangerous card to play, even I'll admit that in my old age, but insofar as I can see at this moment in time everything he lost, we have gained in ways unimaginable."

The youngest wolf shifted a little in his sleep, murmuring and twisting his head to the side. Rosario moved quickly to his nephew and placed a reassuring hand on his head in order to settle the other down. "So you are saying that the girl is—" he started before a finger was placed as fast as lightning onto his lips.

"Not yet, little Roro, not yet," Disreli said with a sigh, removing his finger from the man's lips. "I don't know enough about her yet but something stirs in this wood and if Jared brings back that flower which I already know he will... then maybe we have something far greater on our hands that either of us ever imagined."

Rosario opted to stare at his nephew, wondering if his mother ever realised just how potentially precious he could turn out to be. A faint smile crossed his features, though it was laced with sadness and regret. Of course Meliva would have known about her son, she had been cursed with the life of a Seer and probably knew more about everything that was going on in the world than anyone would have ever suspected. He still missed his sister dearly but had tried to raise her one remaining son in loving memory of her so that she could live on in another form. Whilst he did not share the ability to predict the future like his mother, Fiero did have her strength and determination which tended to make him an over-protective zealot, but that was just the way the boy was.

"I don't think it's a case of not knowing, brother," Rosario said, turning back to the old werewolf. "It's a case of not having anything confirmed. Meliva sought to protect him best out of all of her cubs despite loving them all to the ends of the Earth and dying in that flaming mess for them."

Nodding at that statement, knowing that his sister would never play favourites in that way, Disreli glanced at the boy whom he had watched grow from a timid and often terrified cub into a cheeky rascal with a strong heart and then finally into a young, able warrior searching for something that he could not possibly have any idea about. "Any word on the boy's father?" he asked, not meaning to change subject so rashly but talk of Meliva made the question bump itself against the inside of his head.

"Not since his last birthday," Rosario replied automatically with a frown. "Well, nothing directly to Fiero anyway. We did receive a package from him around two months ago but we haven't opened it." Lightly the alpha of the pack sighed, shaking his head. "It is addressed to him alone and has one of those locks upon it so that only he may open it. We were thinking it would be best to keep it until his First Moon Celebration, since it is on February 29th."

A shiver of dread passed through Disreli and his eyes opened wide in fear for a second, like some evil thought had just struck him. "Two weeks from today? How can that be so?"

"His twenty-first birthday was just last month on the 29th, Disreli, you were there," Rosario stated, not understanding the significance. "There will be his first full moon as an adult on that date. Stefina thought that it would be the best time for him to–"

The old wolf let out a very long sigh. "I know all of that, it is just that if things are as they appear then I dread to think..." Catching himself, the old wolf looked rather guiltily at Rosario before coughing gently. "Take me to see the girl, then I will know if my fears are justified or if they are just the misguided musings of one who is far too old to chew at the bones of life."

Slowly the younger brother nodded and stepped up next to Disreli to help ease him up onto his old shaky legs. He did not know the significance of the date but something about the old man's mannerisms suggested that it was a very important day.

However, before they could even begin to try and reach the door where the girl was currently being held, Stefina stepped directly in their path looking ever the protective mother. "Where do you two presume you are going?" she asked, her tone suggesting very clearly that right at this second, she was the one who was in charge and no amount of pleading or begging was going to get anyone out of trouble or for her to move out of the doorway.

Rosario couldn't help but grin at recognising his mate's protective tendencies just a fraction before coughing gently to steal his wife's attention and also hopefully calm her wrath.

"Disreli wants to see the girl who was brought here, Stefina," he spoke gently, hoping that she would just shrug in her usual manner and allow them passage.

Instead, her hands went straight to her hips. "I already told you no, and I will stick by that statement. She's nowhere near even close to being awake, let alone having much of a chance to answer any of your questions."

The eldest werewolf held up his hand. "My dear Stefina, I will not disturb the girl from her slumber, I merely wish to look in upon her for a few precious seconds just to see if I recognise her or not."

"Recognise her?" The words echoed back though they were lost on Disreli's ears who had used the single second of distraction to slip past his sister-in-law and push open the door that was just behind her. His speed amazed the two younger wolves enough for them both to remain stock still and forget to go after him.

Disreli took a few faltering steps into the room, feeling harsh and bitter tears sting at the corner of his eyes. The young woman who lay on the bed was fairly plain and simple to look at with skin that was just a little too far past the point of pale covering a thin, petite frame. Her hair was a dirty black, in desperate need of a wash and dry through to make it shimmer like silk. If truth be told a bath would do her the world of good, removing the layers upon layers of dirt and grime which clung to the fair skin and took away the effect of her soft, pleasing lines. Reaching forth, his old fingers brushed along her arm, cracking a small piece of dried mud and blood off in the process so that it cascaded to the floor below. His old eyes focused on the patch of newly exposed skin and the glow which issued forth.

It was a faint white light, more of a reflection than an actual glow but shimmering beautifully in the strangeness of this plain setting. The glow came from the end of an elegant swirl that traced its way up her arm and around her face, he remembered them so well for they had always shone so brightly in the darkest part of the long, horrible nights spent trying to survive under the oppressive forces of Cresta Du Winter's ever-present watchful eye. It had been many, many long years since he had seen those beautiful swirls and even when covered with a blanket, the old wolf knew exactly where each one began and ended. He sighed, long and hard, a sigh filled with so much love and so much regret that it was hard to believe anything could be corrected in this man's life ever again.

Disreli leaned close, pressing his lips to her forehead and lightly closed his eyes. "You are safe now, my little one, I will make up for all the time that I left you behind in the hands of that monstrous woman."

Gently he pulled away from the still slumbering figure, choosing not to elaborate on his words as he turned back to the silent watchers at the door. "A necklace?"

Stefina rallied first. "Pardon?"

"A necklace," Disreli repeated himself. "Did she have a necklace about her person?"

Silently nodding, the alpha female scurried quickly away down the corridor to the airing cupboard to pull out a folded towel. "It was caked in mud, blood and a thousand other substances. I cleaned it to the best of my ability and placed it in here to dry so the metal wouldn't corrode."

Opening the layers with expert fingers, the gold and diamond-set cross pendant shimmered in the halogen of the light above their heads. It was a Celtic cross, woven delicately in gold and set with small shimmering diamonds that almost bloomed like flowers.

"Isn't that...?" Rosario turned to glance at Disreli who nodded solemnly before lifting the pendant and chain from the towel.

Carefully he turned it over in his fingers and murmured an inscription on the back before placing the cross back on the towel. "Once the girl is awake, I will send for her after a time. She will be confused and distrusting at first as is to be expected by all those who wake up in the kindness of strangers but I know that she will not wish to leave this place. For now, I must retire. Good day to you both."

Watching the old wolf as he shuffled his way along the corridor, husband and wife turned their attention to one another after he had rounded the corridor and presumed that he had headed towards his own large room towards the back of the Den.

"What is going on, Rosario?" Stefina asked her voice low and quiet with intrigue but also a tinge of fear as it was not usual for the elder wolf to speak of such things in the way that he just did, "and what is this?"

Rosario swallowed gently, purely to make sure that his voice was still fully-functioning. "It's a pendant that once belonged to a priest by the name of Father Tuxbury. He was a member of the Hunters."

"Was?"

"He left on good terms in order to raise a child." Carefully Rosario reached out and also took the pendant, flipping it over to read the inscription on the back. "The moon and sun bear you no ill, my dearest daughter."

Stefina felt a shudder go through her system. "Just who have we taken into our Den, Rosario?"

For a few seconds, the alpha male was silent as if forming the words in his head or trying to make a very difficult decision. His blue eyes narrowed and the stump of his left ear twitched in very high concern. "Possibly a child who could remake the world into a much greater place or be the start of its total destruction."

Chapter 4

Maiden and Knight

The hills stretched out as far as the eye could see, great towering pinnacles of dark greens, browns and that strange blue colour that the natural darkness of night time brought to the world. Fiero had the strangest feeling that he knew these hills and valleys exceptionally well but could not recall from where. But what was more disconcerting at that moment in time was the fact that the well-trodden path before and behind him was also well known to him, not once had he found himself inexplicably lost since setting out from the Inn despite there only being a few stars to direct his way in the darkness. Not even the moon was showing itself tonight, which was strange as he was sure it had been nearly full yesterday but the werewolf brushed it off as simply one of his many mistaken observations that frequently occurred.

Reaching the pinnacle of the climb, the dark-haired boy stopped once again to stare across the land and found himself thinking just how magnificently empty it all felt during the long slumber. How much longer would he have to endure the silent beauty of the night without that special someone beside him, calling forth the sweet harmonies that brought a new kind of vibrant life into the world around him. Yes, there were many beautiful views to see in the world, many dazzling creations of man and creature alike that dominated the scenery and gave it a purpose and meaning but they held little of the old times, the history that created them nor the gentleness of the thousands of lives that had sculpted the landscape over the vast number of generations. It was all locked away, hidden in the midst of long-forgotten memories and withered old documents.

Fiero was just about to start questioning himself in regards to these strange and complicated thoughts, which were running around his head when sharply his ear flicked to the side and he snapped his head to the left as a horse came galloping by. The rider apparently did not see his attempt to get out of the way, nor heard his angry yell of frustration in his general direction but a mere four seconds after he had passed Fiero saw why. An arrow, hawthorn shafted with an entwining black string whistled through the air and slammed neatly into the back of the man whom Fiero now noted was dressed in the garbs of a priest. Watching the man fall as if in slow motion, the werewolf barely noticed the approach of the group of vampires until they were almost on top of him but they ignored his presence.

"We know you are there," said the one who must have fired the arrow as he was carrying a bow made out of the same material which quite frankly looked so out of place by his side that Fiero couldn't help but feel annoyed with his mere presence. "Step out quietly and we will not harm you."

Turning his murky blue eyes onto the scene, feeling just the slightest pinprick of pain in the corner of each one, Fiero blinked upon seeing a child, no more than six-years-old at best, slowly pick herself up out of the arms of the man who had fallen. She looked so desperately thin and ailing that he immediately felt sorry for her but it was a greater sorrow of understanding the pain in her eyes that stared levelly at the vampires in front of her. "You will not hold your word," the girl said, her voice straining because of the tears in her eyes and a trickle of blood, which was rolling down from the corner of her mouth, "for my mother has forbidden such a thing. I will not come with you willingly; never shall I come to you bidding."

The vampires chuckled, the one with the bow smirking to himself before striding towards the girl he towered over. "Then unwillingly it shall be, little freak. Come here and let's see what you're made of."

It was at that second that the child's amber eyes fell directly onto Fiero's and anger boiled over in the werewolf. "You get away from her!" he yelled, lunging for the vampire with all of his strength and a growl which would have outdone the earliest wolf howls in the night. The vampires reacted to him in a panic, like they were unable to see him despite their supernatural abilities and Fiero fully used that to his advantage. Five in all were they strong and within a minute of leaping into the fray, only the bow wielder still remained alive having moved faster than the others in order to grab the girl in an attempt to flee.

But a sharp whistle from the enraged werewolf saw the horse which the man had been riding charge at the vampire and send him flying backwards straight into the all too willing claws. "When you meet your maker, vampire," Fiero hissed in the man's ear, "tell him that there is only one in the mortal lands who can ever hurt her and it shall never come to pass whilst I stand by her side!" His claws ripped through

40

flesh and bones, tearing the monster apart in a shower of blood and dust which was carried away on a sharp wind. Breathing heavily, Fiero paused finally to try and work out what had just occurred before feeling a small hand rest in his own before the world was filled with ash and smoke.

Ekata stared up at the large country house with its sandy-coloured walls and plain white windows and wondered vaguely how she had gotten to such a place. Her feet ached with pain and she was breathing heavily but it seemed almost impossible that she had walked any great distance. The house gave off a warm feeling, the kind of place where a strong and closely knit family lived all together enjoying one another's company. It was unlike any other home she had seen on her long travels, there were few secrets and hardly any malicious lies kept in this house she could see all too easily but her instincts were also telling her that this was no human household. It smelt distinctly of wolves.

The stars above twinkled faintly in the sky, but there was no moon to guide by, not that the gentle glow of lights hadn't been hard to trace of course. Carefully pushing open the little wooden gate, her tired body pushed its way towards the house, noting that the garden whilst plain and simple, was kept beautifully with just the right amount of flowers and vegetable patches to balance the huge expanses of playing areas that young cubs would inevitably need. There were even flowers around the doorway, growing together in a thick clump of intertwining branches that shimmered gently in the light from the nearest windows. Some part of her heart felt at home here, like this was a place where she could truly belong but the thought of such a thing made next to no sense to her in the slightest. She was a Volf, something unlovable that would never be accepted anywhere by anyone as she had been told many times.

Just thinking that it would be best to leave, Ekata nearly jumped out of her skin when the front door opened, showering the warm light onto the pathway and herself to reveal a very handsome, if slightly rough around the edges, werewolf alpha with dark brown hair and stunning blue eyes who strode out onto the flagstones followed by his mate. "Please, Germaine, don't go. I fear the worst," the woman said with tears in her eyes, her dark blond hair and misty grey eyes almost a shocking contrast but the watching Volf felt a certain familiarity about the pair which stopped her from apologising and running away.

The alpha sighed and turned back. "If I don't go then we run the greater risk of losing everything, I will not roll over and be treated like a dog by the likes of them."

"I'm not asking you to do anything like that at all." The woman despite showing a fragility that was clearly unusual for her, was strong and determined with a fierce understanding of the world. "I just want to know that you will come back in one piece. Please, my brothers will be here before tomorrow's nightfall."

Germaine turned his attention back to her, placing a kiss on her lips. "By tomorrow we could have lost everything. I will come back for you, I promise."

Without even understanding why, Ekata knew that he would never be coming back to this wonderful little house and as he passed her, she reached out her hand as though to block his leaving. Expecting to be completely ignored, the girl was surprised to see the wolf stop for a few seconds and glance at her before smiling sadly as if he knew so much more than he was willing to say. "Thank you," he whispered before turning and disappearing into the blackness of the garden. Before the Volf could even begin to try and comprehend what had just happened there was a sudden explosion of light from behind her and she twisted around to find the entire building engulfed in flames.

There were screams all around but she could barely focus on any details as only dark shadows moved back and forth across the red and orange dance of the fire. She couldn't predict how much time had passed but all she knew was that whoever had done this had been malicious about it. All of the windows on the lower ground floor had been boarded up with thick heavy oak panels and the door was wedged in the same style. To make it worse however there was a pit dug around the house, only about a foot deep that was filled with a vile-smelling oil which burned a scorching white colour. The entire family was trapped inside the house, that much she knew and understood but all that filled her was a terror of losing something so precious that without consciously being aware of what she was doing until it was too late, Ekata found herself running through the flames and straight into the burning building.

It was only later that she wondered how she had managed to pass through the very solid burning wood and bricks or why the figures standing around the house were dressed in heavy black robes, which were marked with saffron-coloured crosses had not seen her but right at that second she was merely running with a purpose that even she herself could not fully comprehend. Every room was alight with the deadly flames and the stairs had long since collapsed before she could even think of heading that way. Screams filled the air, children screaming for their mother, elders within the pack trying to find a way out and the anguished cry of a mother losing everything that was most important to her in the entire world.

Rushing towards that heartbreaking sound, Ekata found the alpha female from earlier clutching a dagger in her heart and staring at a man who seemed unaffected by the flames advancing upon a boy of possibly eight years old with a glistening steel blade that looked viciously curved and wicked. "To save the world, you must pass over to the next one now," the figure said, also dressed in the same black cloaks as the others but with a notable white bandana tied around his head. The little boy was backed up against the hearth, shaking terribly with fear watching as the blade was raised high and then slashed down low. A deep, terrible and bloody cut was caused across the child's abdomen, running from his right shoulder to his left hip which caused him to scream out in pain and terror before attempting to run.

The swordsman growled his frustration, wondering how his aim could have been thrown off and wildly he slashed at the boy's back, halting the transformation to a natural wolf form and causing a similar scar, which mirrored the direction and position of the first one.

Crashing to the floor the boy crawled desperately, unable to see the shimmering barrier which had formed around him, his mind too caught up with the death and destruction that he was suddenly witnessing. "You cannot survive! Accept your fate and all of this will end," the man growled lunging forward to grab the boy, with murderous intent in his eyes. Ekata dropped the barrier she had been holding over the boy, her terror at the situation having caused the delay in the activation of it, and instead grabbed the bandana the man was wearing, pulling his head back sharply before slamming him backwards into the opposite wall.

Looking stunned, the man tried to locate his attacker but only saw the boy who was withering on the floor. "You foolish child, no creature has the right to wield that power!" he shouted, pushing himself forward whilst raising his sword to charge once again at the boy and this time make the blow count. He barely made it five paces before finding himself literally frozen to the core as a blade made of ice was sank straight into his heart. "Who are you to say what he can do and what he can't?" Ekata whispered in a bittersweet tone in his ear. "He has more right than you to wield the power that you tried to steal. He is mine and nothing you do will ever take him from me."

Barely aware that she had moved, Ekata found herself outside in the garden of the house, holding onto the terrified child who was weeping openly. Glancing down at him, she gently rested her hand on his head, desperate to know his name but then a soft darkness hit her and for a time she knew no more.

Pulling himself up from the log he had been resting on, Fiero was surprised to find himself on the edges of the Marshes near his home, but yet there was a different feeling in the air. Normally the place reeked of death and forewarning, a place where few fools dared to tread even in the direst of circumstances as one misplaced step and it was down to the bottom of the depths to join the long-forgotten dead. However right now it smelt more like a lily pond, with a fresh running spring nearby replenishing the water constantly though unseen by all eyes. There were even small glistening flowers on the surface, small and delicate and just about to begin prying open their petals as the sun began to rise in the east. The last few eager fireflies hovered around in shimmering bright lights and twirled about lazily as they prepared to find shelter.

There was a fine peace in the air, reminding him of the midsummer night festivities that his aunt and uncle held and the glorious feeling of the summer being in full swing. A time of joy, for life to be good and families to be happy before they started to gather the necessaries in order to survive the winter that was coming.

It was then that his ears twitched lightly upon hearing a song being sang so gently that it sounded more like the passing of the breeze than words. Carefully he made his way through the water, not aware of the silver trace which was slowly forming around him, and headed in the direction of the sound. He had no idea why he was drawn to such a thing but in his heart he knew that he had to reach the singer, though why was a mystery.

The sun was well up by the time he reached the bend that led to the river and for a second he paused, remembering acutely how he had been running wildly not two nights ago around this area and had tumbled down from this very spot. His smoky grey eyes searched the land in front of him for anything to explain his sudden descent towards the river but instead they were captured by something else.

Sitting with her back to him, was a young female dressed in a flowing ivory-white gown that reminded him of a painting he had discovered quite by accident in the basement of the Den. It had been held just in the cover of an old, battered and torn-looking book and was not much bigger than a postcard. The painting contained two figures, one male who stood tall and proud in a dark flowing black and gold suit fit for any prince whilst the other was female in the white gown. He had found himself most disappointed that either figure had many details other than the clothes they wore but had not investigated further on the matter.

Of course he had read through the book, of what he could decipher of it, and found that it told a story of a Silver Maiden who was said to be born into the world as a child of sorrow but would ultimately either become the guiding light of rebirth or the inevitable fall into darkness for the whole supernatural world. At the time the young werewolf had been confused over such a matter, as it seemed impossible to him that any child could be born that way but then the tale had begun to speak of a Guardian Knight who would find the Maiden, though his path to her would be littered with many sorrows of his own and regardless of the outcome of her fate, he would always remain beside her. Fiero had felt strangely calm reading that passage, normally such sissy nonsense would bore him to tears but there was just too much familiarity to the words that he couldn't stop reading.

Though now as he stared at the girl on the riverbed, he reflected keenly on the words now and wondered, not for the first time, if there was more to him than even his uncles suspected. The figure was still sitting in place, singing her little tune and he carefully cast his eyes around until he spotted the old bridge with a path that led down to the riverbed as he did not want to tumble down like a clumsy oaf and spoil the moment. He knew that he had to talk to this girl, for no other reason than to satisfy his curiosity, or at least that was what his head told him whilst his heart began to beat just a little faster in anticipation.

Flicking her ears back upon hearing a sound, Ekata rose swiftly in a panic, presuming that she had lingered far too long and was about to move on when she realised that there was no freezing snow or biting ice in this place. Slowly her amber eyes took in the riverbank with its twisting roots of ancient trees and soft, clay like mud but not recognising it fully at first.

There was a softness here, like the awakening of the world after a well-needed downpour of rain and a distant hint of home-baked bread and wild flowers pruned back in a beautiful garden drifted on the breeze. It was safe here, there were no lingering threats of vampires or hunters or insane monsters spurred up from the blackest parts of the blackest caves in the worlds of creation looming ever-present and for a moment she felt the uttermost joy of being free.

Except for a doubt that naturally lingered in her mind about having been here before, in the snow and cold, covered in mud and terrified out of her mind. Taking a couple of steps towards the babbling waters, just becoming aware of how high the sun was up in the sky now, she stared into them as if looking for some form of answer. Pulling up sharply from the water, her breath catching in her throat at the reflection which she presumed at first was some form of illusion, Ekata blinked a few times before leaning back down. A silver moon shone in place of the sun and the stars twinkled high above and the figure looking terrified back at her was caked with mud and so many tear lines that it looked like two marks had been purposefully made on her face. She knew it was her own reflection but couldn't comprehend why it had shocked her so much. Her appearance was never much of a thing to remark upon unless it was merely to be called a thousand more terrible names for it. But here was little time to work on one's appearance when trying to escape from blood-thirsty vampires who were after your throat.

It was then that the waters stilled long enough for her to see fully why she had been so shocked by the image, there was another figure with her. He was slumped on the opposite bank, looking like he had gone through a war but was clearly still alive and very much well. The other her in the water nodded before retreating back to the boy and a fish's bright back broke the surface of the mirror like water and shattered it. Pulling back with a confused frown, the girl's hands immediately sought for the cross that she bore around her neck normally to seek the advice of Father Tuxbury despite the fact that he had been dead longer than she ever cared to remember. Clutching at the empty space where it normally hung, Ekata panicked for a few seconds before suddenly catching sight of her arm. Instead of the rags she was used to wearing, there was an elegantly long silk sleeve that flowed down from just below her shoulder for the full length of her arm.

Before she could ask aloud her questions of confusion, there was a snap of a twig being broken behind her and quickly she snapped around, expecting to find a vampire waiting to pounce. Instead her eyes widened in pleasant surprise when they fell on the figure of a young knight or possibly rouge it was hard to tell, who stared at her with stunning silver eyes, whilst the full-grown coal-black wolf ears clearly marked him as being a creature of the night world. He was dressed in a rough leather tunic and black trousers, his messy brown hair having been semi-tamed but in a way which would fall out the first opportunity that was presented and his bare arms looked formidable but also warm and inviting.

Blinking, she heard Father Tuxbury's voice in her head whispering, "One day you will find your knight, my most beautiful child, and he will find you. Though you may not know one another now, when the time comes you will see past the outward appearance and into his very soul for you have been connected far longer than even the greatest of scholars can predict."

Aware that the young man in front of her had said something, she tilted her head to the side in question, her white ears flicking back and forth. Fiero couldn't help but smile at the action, as it caused the woman in front of him to appear childlike and sweet to an almost irresistible level which normally would have disturbed him. She was more beautiful than he had ever imagined the final painting to be, with her long ebony-black hair and strange amber-coloured eyes. Part of him thought that she looked like a doll, one that should be kept in a beautiful case to be viewed but never touched by anyone but the majority of his mind couldn't help but be blinded by an overwhelming sense of joy and a love which shouldn't yet be possible.

Stepping closer to the girl, who only flinched just a little in his presence, his hand rose steadily to her cheek, the backs of his fingers running down the uttermost smoothness as he breathed out steadily for a second or two. "I found you, my lady, just as I promised I would do."

Ekata blinked up at him, recalling the words from the other night and understanding them more without understanding anything else in the grand picture that was around them. "You should have looked more carefully when you came to find me," she said teasingly towards him, like she had always known this stranger but not questioning it now.

A smirk was her reward, the dark type of knowing that was sarcastic and yet wonderfully sincere as her hands reached out cautiously to rest against his broad chest and shoulders, "I was beginning to fear I would never find your rebirth, I feared that the darkness had already claimed you."

"It tried," Fiero whispered back, finding his arms winding around her small frame. "But it shall take more than them fools to destroy either one of us."

Pulling him just a little closer, the Volf had to pause just for a second before kissing him. "Tell me your name, sir knight, so I will not forget it upon awakening."

"You already know it, my dearest Ekata," Fiero whispered, only reflecting later how he had known hers without having ever hearing it, before placing a kiss lightly on the soft and waiting lips.

When he pulled back, he heard the whisper of, 'Fiero', before the sunlight suddenly became overbearing and with a groan he found himself awake, in his old bedroom in the Den with his aunt pushing open the curtains of his room.

Sitting up a little too quickly, the werewolf shook his head in order to dispel the wave of dizziness that hit him before glancing up at Stefina when she approached with that worried expression on her face. "Where's Ekata?" he asked almost instantly, before correcting himself, "the girl that was brought here. Where is she?"

Carefully stepping back from her nephew, Stefina seemed to shudder before quietly stepping out of the room and closing the door behind her. Fiero frowned but opted to not cause any more hassle than what he had clearly done already. It was only then that he caught his reflection in the mirror and saw that just for a moment his eyes shone silver before returning to their normal odd colouring.

Chapter 5

Crescent Moon

Gently twisting a slither of just-cooked meat around his fingers, Mephistopheles regarded the Den with bored eyes. It was like most typical Den's, a small, rather dilapidated house that barely looked like it could hold more than five people at best which had been situated in a place where its presence would go unremarked. Forests were typical of Werewolves, as it made sense for there to be old houses in the middle of them and it was rare for anyone to come knocking as most ramblers had their own routes already pre-planned on little paths marked out by other humans. He did have to begrudgingly admit that this pack had definitely a sense of pride and survival by housing themselves so close to a rather lethal-looking marsh which indubitably had many horror stories that were, for once, actually true but it did complicate things a little for him and his sister. "Crafty swine's, the lot of them," he murmured quietly to himself, blinking his grey eyes slowly as if thinking a multitude of different thoughts.

Siren was thankfully distracted enough by the fire and was in the process of tormenting a squirrel she had managed to capture so was not paying any real attention to her big brother's actions. Not that there was anything to pay attention to of course, Mephistopheles reflected that was what made life so much easier with the only female member of Cresta's vampiric brood but even the great amongst the great sometimes had to take account of the bigger picture. Especially when it came to tricky siblings.

His grey eyes roamed over the visible building, trying to gauge just how far below the soil the Den would go and how many tunnels would lead off of it. Or whether or not the pack more up on the times and living in a denser situation, more like a house which had been built underground with natural light pools and hidden windows? Impossible to tell from the old cottage that was the surface structure but knowing would make life all the easier.

Plus, if they went back without the Volf, then Cresta's wrath would be the least of their worries. The tricky little girl had managed to get herself firmly inside the barriers, which prevented them from entering but also meant that until her feeding she would be trapped inside. That would be fun to watch, part of his mind reflected, seeing the reaction of these placid wolves as they realised just what they were harbouring under their roof whilst one of their own was drained in front of their eyes. Vampires needed blood to stay alive, as did both Volf's but their hunger was far greater and usually came on without warning. Unless one knew the true meaning of the Blood Moon.

There was a squeak behind him, followed by a sudden scampering noise and quietly he turned, upraising a midnight-blue eyebrow up at his sister who was standing just at the edge of the firelight with her back to him. Her long auburn hair cascaded down her back in a mess that still somehow managed to look enticing, whilst the folds of her dress looked more frayed than ever before. "Squirrel gone," came the reply to the unasked question, which caused the older vampire to lightly roll his eyes and turn his attention back to the house.

"Must you always play with your food?"

Siren turned, smirking towards her older brother as she sidled up towards him and gently wrapped her arms around his own. "You mean like the way you do with that little thing that's caught up in there?" Childish innocence poured out of the tone, accompanied by the strange little girlish laugh that beguiled the worrying amount of self-delusional temperament that was a mark of Siren's otherness in the realm of others.

"This is different," Mephistopheles said, for once not shaking her off his arm like some contagious monster which genuinely surprised the girl though she managed to think wisely of not commenting on such a thing. "I don't intend to eat that freak in any way, shape or form."

"But you'll steal her powers," Siren said, hugging just a little closer. "You'll even steal them from Mother just to ensure that you rise above her."

There was a snort towards the comment, though whether in contempt or agreement it was hard to say. For a second, the girl found herself recalling a softer time when things at home had been wonderful and so much simpler. How the dangerous vampire she was currently clinging to had always been so soft and gentle with her, doing anything he could in order to help her survive the strangeness of the world. Siren knew she was different, knew that there was something wrong with her but had never been able to work out just what. Yet her eldest brother had always been there for her, putting little notes on things to help her identify them, rushing around for hours in order to catch her in order to go to bed or just quietly sitting by the fire with her reading stories aloud. "I would steal the powers of the gods themselves and give them to you, my most sweet sister, as mother holds no power in comparison to me. She cannot ever wield the power of the Silver Maiden nor the Golden Prince, despite having the talent to be able to bring forth their powers from their current hosts."

Siren twisted to look at her brother, for a second believing to see him in a different light or that someone else had spoken on his behalf but the illusion was spoiled mere seconds later when the older male shoved her roughly off. "Go and see if you can find some Werewolf to play with," he stated his voice cold and devoid of any real emotion. "Do try and bring him back alive though. We need to learn the layout of this place and fast." Mephistopheles watched his sister go about her duty with her usual demented flare and smiled sadly at the thought that she had already forgotten those wonderful moments they had shared together. His green eyes turned back on the house, flickering in the firelight. "Soon, Ekata, soon... you will be back in my hands. Whether you want to be or not."

~

Blinking open her amber eyes, Ekata winced initially at the burning sunlight before gently rolling over onto her side. A ripple of a frown crossed her features as the usual searing pain from her side simply ached dully. Her eyes arched downwards to find her body covered with a hand-made blanket that smelt of mint leaves which had small moons and stars embroidered onto it. Sitting up a little, with just a minor wince of pain, the Volf stared in amazement at her arms, which were clean, and wrapped around the various scars, cuts, and grazes were a series of clean, cotton bandages. The faint scent of homemade healing ointments still lingered on her skin but they were pleasant smells, laced with lavender and honey suckle. The rest of her body had also been treated, a few of the deeper wounds carefully stitched up before being covered with more of the protective bandages.

It had been so long since she had felt such little pain that the sensation was rather alien to her. Actually the very concept of being completely clean was enough to send her into an almost dizzy mindset as her own scent was suddenly very much more present than it ever had been. "We did, Father," she murmured quietly to herself, her fingertips stroking down what she imagined to be a familiar golden chain. "We made it."

At the point where the pendant usually would be, however, Ekata was shocked to find only plain clean skin and in a panic she glanced around the room trying to find it. However, her attention was once again distracted by the simplicity of the room that she did not recognise or know in the slightest. It could be conceived to be a guest bedroom, with a reasonably sized double bed, a little dressing table and a chest of drawers for storing of clothes with just a few little knick-knacks here and there to give it a presence of being used at other times. Her eyes were drawn to a small vase of flowers on the little windowsill and without considering much, she drew herself out of the bed with relatively little hassle.

The flowers were artificial blooms in silk blues and greens with a soft white edging. The Volf had no idea what type of flower they were but something about them made a small smile cross her features as her fingers gently rolled over the fine edges. Tilting her head to the side, as she admired them she spotted a flash of red and turned to look. Sitting on the windowsill was a stunning red rose which had been carefully cleared of all of its thorns and it glistened slightly as if it had been sprayed with something to keep it well preserved. Ekata had never seen a rose before, except from a distance, but she understood the meaning behind it. Love.

"Fiero," she whispered gently, wondering where he was before changing the question around to who he was.

For a moment her amber eyes lifted up to look at the woods outside of her window and she thought that she saw a figure standing by the trees, with dark messy hair and eyes that appeared to be unnatural but the next second he was gone from sight and she could not see any sign that he had been there at all.

Her mind was filled with so many confusing thoughts that the sudden appearance of Stefina would have passed her by completely except for the fact that the older woman had hurried across, wrapped a large sheet around her naked form and pulled her hurriedly from the window. "Oh my dear, you mustn't do such things. Whilst I trust all of my boys to behave themselves I very much doubt that even they would be able to resist such a temptation." Her voice was lined with the merriment of motherhood, as well as the worry of it at the same time.

Ekata blinked at the female werewolf, not understanding at first just what was being said to her. A light blush crossed her features upon figuring it out and her head was hung in shame. "Forgive me, I meant no offence."

Stefina stared at the little Volf for a few seconds, noting automatically which bandages would need changing and that her ebony-black hair was glistening after being thoroughly scrubbed clean, as well as the two white wolf ears standing out so much more prominently now. But her keen eyes also picked out the fine swirls of what appeared to be white on her body, they had been present before of course but she had presumed them to be patches of dry skin. Now she could see that they were beautiful, elegant swirls that were captivating. Disreli had seemed to know more about them but had refused to elaborate on any details as he would frequently do.

"None was taken, dear child," Stefina said, stepping in front of the girl. "I guess it is just natural for a mother to over-react to such things. Do you feel better now?"

Ekata glanced up at the woman, a frown on her face that was lined with fear. The older woman just smiled gently at the girl, brushing a few stray strands of hair from her face. "Don't look so worried, you are safe for the time being. One of my sons brought you back to the Den in a terrible state, I can tell you, and I just had to help you to heal. Don't look so scared, young one, we mean you no harm."

The Volf swallowed, looking directly into the other woman's eyes to see the telltale signs of evil intention or illusion. Cresta Du Winter wasn't beyond doing such things and had tricked her many times in the past but there was something so different about this woman that she couldn't even begin to work out what question to ask first. There were many swarming around her mind, all along the lines of who the other woman was, where she was right at this second, why had they helped her, how long has she been here and were her frightful half-brother and sister still lurking on the outskirts of the protective barriers? Though as soon as the question raised itself in her head it was answered as distantly she could feel their strange auras, a trait which at one time she had cherished but now feared beyond all things. Opening her mouth, Ekata selected a question at random. "Where is Fiero?"

Her look of surprise mirrored the werewolf mother's look but thankfully the older woman rallied quicker. "On patrol at the moment." She let out a long breath though of worry or relief it was hard to say. "With his cousins. He probably won't be back until sunset at the very least."

The Volf looked meekly sorry before looking up at Stefina, clearly ready to ask the proper questions that should have been asked before. "To answer, my name is Stefina Fernell and I am the alpha female of this pack. You are currently in our Den which is held in the woods of Kilda far further north than from where you hail from I am led to believe. You were brought here by Jared, my eldest son, on February fifteenth and it is now the twentieth."

"Five days?" Ekata asked, shuddering and shaking her head. "How has it taken them that long?"

She nearly jumped when Stefina placed a gentle hand on her head to stroke her fine hair. "Our defenses are strong, we ensured that a long time ago, my dear. You are safe with us for the time being and no harm will come to you whilst you are in my care. That I can guarantee you."

Already willing to believe this fine woman, Ekata had to stop herself from following through on the urge to throw her arms around this fine-framed figure and begin bawling like a tiny child. There was so much of a loving mother within the werewolf that the little Volf found herself back in her earliest memories when Esmerida had been the one to look after the pair of them. How she had always been full of fun, smiling gently and prepared to put up with the twins' nonsense that frequently came about. Of course, there were vast differences between the two. Esmerida had been an immortal child of just eighteen back then with shimmering blond hair and bright blue eyes whereas Stefina was well over the age of forty by her looks and was a werewolf with a large brood of cubs. Probably several from the way that she was speaking but it did not show on her frame at all. But their essence was the same, the warmth, love and protection that harkened back to the soul and was ever-present no matter what the world threw at them.

But Ekata had been tricked before and couldn't bring herself to trust Stefina just yet, even though she most desperately wanted to do so. "How do I know I can trust you? How can I be certain that you are not affiliated with Cresta and are luring me into a trap to drag me back to that horrible place?"

Stefina's green eyes softened in pity for the girl, almost understanding her pain and fear to a far greater extent than she had ever expected anyone to understand. Rising a hand in a soft movement to wait for a second or so, the red-haired werewolf quickly walked to the door where she picked up a small towel that had been refolded several times. "Because, my dear, my brother-in-law and husband both recognised this precious thing and swore that you were to remain with us no matter what the stakes were." Sitting by the girl again, she opened the layers of the towel to reveal the cross.

Ekata swiftly snatched the chain and held it close, but in a careful enough hold that it would only lightly scald her. Lightly she kissed the diamonds, a look of pure relief rushing through her features and causing the white marks to glow just a little bit brighter. Amber eyes turned to the green ones. "You know what I am?"

"Yes."

"And yet you do not fear me?"

"What do I have to fear?" Stefina took the necklace from the girl's shivering hands and gently clasped it around her neck, ensuring that the cross pendant did not actually touch her skin and lay on the towel instead. "From a girl who has captured the heart of my dearest nephew and has long held the admiration and protection of my husband and brother-in-law?"

"Who are they?" Ekata had to ask, feeling something stir within her heart though unsure as to what it was.

Stefina smiled, remembering a time when an ancient mystic had told her that she would eventually gain a daughter who would be precious to the world but not of her own flesh and blood. "My husband is Rosario Fernell, alpha of the pack, and my brother-in-law is Disreli Fernell, eldest of his line... are you okay, my dear?" Her hands went to steady the Volf who was suddenly shaking, water pooling in her eyes as tears threatened to fall. Without prompting, Stefina quickly pulled the girl into a protective hug, feeling nothing but trust and love radiating from her in return.

"Ekata," the Volf managed to hiccup through her tears., "Ekata Monet. The name they gave me."

Smiling, Stefina cradled her new daughter and gently shushed her whilst silently she began sending prayers of thanks and protection to any gods or goddesses who would listen to her.

~

Walking just behind Stefina, feeling very conscious of herself for the first time in a long while, Ekata took several deep calming breaths in order to steady her nerves. Whilst she knew whom she was going to be talking to, there was still a part of her heart that was fearful that this was another illusion. Though the walk down the corridor did help to relieve that tension as the walls were lined with family photographs ranging from the standard array of grouped poses to the funny single shots that looked strange to her eyes. There were so many pictures all filled with smiling faces that it was hard to ever imagine that sadness had visited this lovely home.

There were lingering traces though, there were only a few pictures of certain members of the vast family and on the left-hand side of one wall there was a little closed cupboard set slightly apart from everything else. A tiny pendant hung from the lowest section, appearing to be a small female figure with wings wrapped around her lithe frame. It twinkled as Ekata took a step towards it and without really understanding why she closed her eyes and raised her hands upwards together in a quick prayer of unheard words before turning her attention swiftly back to Stefina who was signaling that she should come quickly.

Taking only a few seconds to reach the other woman, the feeling of nervousness crept back over her as her sensitive nose caught two scents. The first was of fresh blood from a recent clean kill that had been chilled slightly. It made her fangs itch desperately behind her gums before almost drawing forth though she just managed to control the desperate call. Stefina's hands on her shoulders helped greatly of course but it was still a struggle. The second scent was of a male wolf, laced with pine and leaf mold but also containing a hint of cinnamon and roasting chestnuts. Her amber eyes moved slowly to the figure sat at the table and a stab of pain, fear and joy went through her heart.

Rosario smiled gently at Ekata, feeling his own fears lift upon seeing her awake and looking the healthiest he had ever seen her. Stefina had given her another bath before re-tending to the multiple wounds that the girl had before dressing her in a pale cream summer dress with little yellow flowers on it. Her ebony-black hair had been brushed through and gently pulled back into a simple half ponytail with an old white hair clip to secure it in place. Her amber eyes burned brightly with millions of emotions and her pale skin glowed just a little pinker. The marks were still present, as they always would be and the stunning white of her ears spoke to a time he had been told about since he was a cub. Tuxbury's pendant glimmered in what could be perceived as a welcoming gesture, further helping Rosario to calm his own nerves once again.

Gently he extended his hand to her. "Come, Ekata, we have much to talk about and very little time to do so." The

Volf nodded, stepping closer and taking hold of the all-too familiar hand before quickly wrapping herself around the elder in a tight hug and thanking all she could think of thanking for getting her this day.

Chapter 6

Birds and Bees

Contemplating only a little why he was standing, half hidden in shadows simply watching the strange young girl whom he had sort of brought into the pack, if he hadn't fallen down and knocked himself out on a tree, Fiero found himself unable to focus on anything else. Not even the familiar presence of his aunt and uncle could distract him. It was like his entire world was filled with nothing but her, every last element of his body and soul wanting nothing more than to hold this mysterious girl, tell her that everything was going to be all right and that she would nevermore have a thing to fear.

Not that it was true of course, even a youngster like him knew all too well that the path she had to tread would be one full of fear and distrust but if he could just restore that hope in her then... a tut escaped him, followed by a long sigh. "What am I doing?" Fiero whispered under his breath. "I don't even know her."

Whilst the werewolf understood the necessities of being a werewolf, the culture and the practice that were behind the ancient rituals and traditions, he had never actually paid that much attention to the opposite sex in any great detail. Sure he was still a young man and would take notice like any male would be expected to do so, but in the grand scheme of things, Fiero hadn't even so much as touched a girl in his life. Let alone kissed one. A flurry of a blush crossed his features as those soft images flashed through his mind once more and hurriedly he pulled back, accidentally bumping into one of the many welsh dressers that lined the large kitchen area. In a panic he turned, trying to catch the white and blue plates before they fell and smashed to the floor but heard the quick approaching pace of his aunt and opted to do what any naughty cub would do when caught doing something that they shouldn't be doing. Fiero turned tail and ran as fast as his legs would carry him.

He didn't stop until he was nearly at the other side of the den, skidding half-blindly around a corner and almost barreling into Jared and Michael, his two eldest cousins.

"Whoa there slick," Michael said with a grin, easily latching onto the young man's t-shirt with his huge hands. "What do you think you're doing, running about like a mad thing?"

"Annoy Mam again by any chance?" Jared asked with a smirk, before glancing at his brother and shaking his head. "Don't go choking him, Michael, we need to at least hear his explanation for running like a headless goose."

Fiero sighed and rolled his eyes. "The phrase is headless chicken, you idiot! Besides that, why's he human? I thought you had given up for lent."

Michael nodded, easily recognising the sarcasm that was coming out of his younger cousin's mouth. "Yep, he's annoyed Mam again or done something that would annoy her at the very least." In all respects, Michael looked more similar to his father than Jared did, if it weren't for the mismatched eyes and stronger build, but it was more common to see the teenager as a wolf roaming the den looking for food. Lightly he flicked his cousin's nose. "Else he wouldn't try to change the subject. Besides that, what's this I hear about you running off into the woods after some girl?"

Grey eyes narrowed in warning and a growl almost escaped his lips but thankfully Jared stepped in and split the two apart. "Michael, I told you not to say anything towards him about that."

"I didn't, I just asked." Michael shrugged. "It wasn't like I heard it from you first. Half the pack knows about what the nugget here did the other night, I'm just want to find out which lucky wolf has bagged herself some fine ass from our little cousin."

Giving his brother a little push, Jared flicked his head back silently towards said cousin who had lost the panicked cub face and was slowly appearing to become very angry and distrusting. Even though Michael had said virtually next to nothing offensive, Fiero was reacting as if someone had just insulted his *mate* in front of him. The boy's body was tense, muscles popping ever so slightly and a deadly cold look settled in his eyes. One wrong move and regardless of pack pecking order, Fiero would lash out. However, the next second, the anger was gone, replaced by confusion and a sigh of an apology.

"No need," Michael said, glancing back towards Jared. "I get it. You best give him the talk, Jared, I'll only piss him off all the more and that's the last thing I need."

Jared glared at his brother. "Why me? Surely he can have the talk from dad."

The younger brother shook his head. "When he's preoccupied with a certain someone? Somehow I don't think so. Plus, you explained it well enough to me and Gregory so I think you can more than do so for Fiero."

"Explain what exactly?" Fiero sounded peeved because he did not like being talked about as if he wasn't standing right next to someone. "If you're talking about the birds and the bees, I already know plenty about that thank you very much."

Michael laughed. "I'm not surprised with you sleeping next door to Matilda."

Jared shook his head, smiling slightly. "But do you know about how you find your mate and everything that goes with becoming her one and only mate?"

There was a pause, clearly the wolf before them was thinking over his response before silently shaking his head. Whilst Fiero knew the basics that were told to him as a child, he had never actually given much thought about the whole process in the grand scheme of things. He had just presumed that his instincts would kick in and everything would be plain sailing from there, but clearly life wasn't going to be that easy on him.

"Thought as much," Jared said, glancing back up the tunnel. "Why don't you come out on patrol with me, Fiero. I'll tell you what I can; it may help you out a fair old bit."

For a moment the still technically considered cub thought about declining but caved in when he thought back to how he had reacted to a simple question about the girl. He needed things set straight in his head before he could start resolving all of the questions in it and the last thing he wanted on his conscience was the fact he had hurt one of his beloved cousins without really understanding as to why he had done it. "Okay... but I still hate patrols," he said, trying to sound sulky but failing drastically.

"Yeah, I know, but trust me..." Jared grinned. "You'll want to be alone for a while after you hear what I've got to say."

~ ~

The forest that surrounded the Den was sparse at the best of times, even in the middle of a blazing hot summer it could be described as uncharitably dead to the world. The trees seemed to half-heartedly give up on growing their leaves, producing only small foliage that aged quicker than most of the surrounding areas and dried up long before the fall season. The local villagers had always put it down to the huge bogs and swamps around the land, presuming that it sucked all the moisture out of the trees and rendered them virtually useless.

Some of the bolder ones told stories of darker things, creatures and witches that lived deep in the woods and stopped anything from growing to ward off intruders but they were tales to enthrall children and tourists for the most part with little substance behind them.

Not that some hadn't paid heed and headed into the forest over the course of the years, there were some hikers who just wouldn't take warnings in the slightest and the local mountain rescue team cursed the days when they had to fetch someone from the bogs. Only once had Fiero known the pack to assist with a rescue, but that had apparently been under special circumstances and he had been far too young at the time to really understand what was going on or remember it properly.

So emerging from the twisted darkness that was the wood to suddenly find a lush, green and very much growing glen, Fiero had to simply stare in amazement. "This is where everything happened?"

Jared nodded. "Yeah... I came by here a couple of days ago and it's expanded since then. It didn't even reach old mother oak there." The wolf pointed to the large oak which had a strange sort of face that had naturally occurred as it had grown. "At least she seems happier now."

Fiero looked at the oak carefully, remembering how he had always been highly scared of it when he was a cub because the face had almost been a scowl, as if the old tree was dissatisfied with something. But now there appeared to be a softening and the beginnings of a smile forming that made the old oak appear at peace after a long time.

Without really thinking, the young cub clambered down into the newer natural glen and let his senses roam. In all his years in the forest he had never smelt something so sweet and wonderful, even the times when his aunt would bring flowers and potted plants home to brighten up the place as she would put it, and the feeling of new life was wonderful.

He spotted the place where he had fallen, where the strange girl had kissed him and instinctively he moved towards it, kneeling down. In his place were a series of white flowers, beautiful and simplistic with a light feathery touch.

"They're called Aquila." Jared's voice cut into Fiero's silence., "Extraordinarily rare and most definitely not native to this area in the slightest. They started turning up shortly after..." sense kicked in and Jared sighed long and hard, suddenly understanding why his father had so many misgivings about this whole adventure. However, before Jared could speak another word, the young werewolf frowned. "Bloody hell."

"What?" Fiero blinked at his cousin, trying to work out just what had freaked the other out.

"Your eyes really are silver." The words were spoken straight, with no levels of joking in them and at an even more confused glance from Fiero continued with, "Take a look in the water. You'll see what I mean."

Feeling a little more than unsure, mainly because his cousins were good at pulling tricks on him, Fiero complied only because he wanted to turn around to the other and tell him off for being such an idiot. So it came as a rather big shock when he saw his reflection and the silver eyes that replaced the grey-blue. Fiero pulled himself back in shock, then looked back into the water and shook his head. "No, it can't be... how?"

"Easy," Jared said, stepping up to the younger boy and gently pulling him back from the water. "Breathe, Fiero, last thing I need is for you to have a heart attack on me."

"But!"

"I know," Jared said, forcing the other to sit down. "It's scary but something is going on here, something important but you've got my dad to guide you and Uncle Disreli as well. Don't panic, we can get through this."

The cub shook for a few long seconds, hanging his head and breathing heavily. He didn't know what was going on, he couldn't even begin to work out what this all meant. Ever since his twenty-first birthday things had rapidly changed, far faster than he had ever suspected that they would and he just had no clue as to where his life was taking him. He could barely keep track of the world around him and now that this strange girl had appeared in his life. Slowly his shoulders relaxed, thinking of the girl whom he only knew by the name of Ekata and felt his heart beat more gently now. Even though he had only briefly been in her arms and watched her from afar, he knew what he felt for her, though couldn't understand.

"Jared," Fiero said gently. "What happens when a werewolf finds their true mate? Even if they've never met except in strange dreams?"

"The latter part you're going to have to work out yourself," Jared said gently, "but I'll tell you about the first part. Though you have to trust me and not freak out too much, because whether you like it or not, I think—"

Fiero nodded. "I just want to know; I don't want to start believing in a lie. That would hurt her more than anything."

There were almost tears in the wolf's voice and Jared unaccustomedly pulled the boy into a hug and held him there, trying to give him strength and courage in what would be a very strange time for the boy. Fiero wasn't one to take such things, he only ever really accepted them from Stefina and that was on extraordinarily rare occasions but tonight however, he latched firmly onto Jared like his life depended on it.

The elder of the two paused, trying to think how best to describe everything and decided to just start as he meant to go on. "Fiero, are you a virgin?"

"Excuse me?"

"Are you a virgin?"

"What's that got to do with any of this?" Fiero asked, looking rather annoyed at his older cousin.

Jared had the decency to at least grimace a little bit. "Well, it has a lot to do with it actually, an awful lot. It can affect you in many different ways, this whole 'true mate' business but if you're prepared then... it's a little easier to deal with. Not a lot, but it makes some things just more realistic." Gently he tilted his head to the side. "So, tell me the truth now, are you a virgin or not?"

For a moment Fiero was silent, clearly deciding how best to state his situation. "Not entirely—"

"Fiero you've either done it with a girl or you haven't. There's no in-between." He sighed. "And if you say that you've fooled around with someone but not actually put any parts of your body together other than your tongues then you are still a virgin."

"Really?"

Nodding, the other smiled. "Yup."

"Damn."

"Don't take it too much to heart." Jared smiled. "Just be thankful that you're not going to have a lot of explaining to do later to me old mam."

A sly grin crossed his features. "I bet you had a few tales to tell on your brothers and sisters."

Jared chuckled. "Oh, she knew all about us lot had us virtually down to the day and who so it was no big deal really. Well, maybe excluding Matilda but you know how that one worked out." Slowly he sighed. "But you always seemed to be in her blank spot for some odd reason, she could never quite work things out with you."

Slowly the wolf sighed. "I don't think I could ever work things out with me."

"But anyway, we're getting off topic." Jared gently cleared his throat. "I'm going to presume that you know all about sex and everything, 'cause there ain't no way in hell that you've been given a sheltered upbringing in the slightest."

"Got the photos to prove it, too."

"Fiero!"

"Sorry."

Biting back a sigh, Jared glared at his younger cousin. "Basically finding a mate is like finding that one really rare and special person in your entire life. No one really knows how it all works but it's instinctual within us wolves... we may pick up a scent from afar or hear their voice on the wind one day and our very core fills up to the brim."

"Even if you've never met?"

There came a nod. "Think of it like the humans, love at first sight. For them it's a complicated situation that doesn't always prove to be right in the slightest. For us wolves though, the second that we find our true mates it's love, lust, jealousy, anger and everything all rolled straight into one powerful emotional state."

Fiero zoned out slightly on his cousin's further explanations, trying to focus his own emotions and how they fitted in with the other's description. He knew that he cared for the strange girl whom he had never met, knew that he had asked for her when he had first woken up from those strange dreams. Everything in his life suddenly seemed to be revolving around her, despite having never met her before and the connection felt so deep and so natural that in the grand scheme of everything that was going on he couldn't deny what he felt. But what did he feel exactly, he wanted to protect the girl, guard her against the evil of the world and stave off any other male who came within fifty yards of her that wasn't family and to him that was more of a brotherly thing to do. It was treating her with affection, with kindness which clearly hadn't been given to her too much in the grand scheme of life.

Was that what was going on between them? Was he turning into a protective big brother for her?

Suddenly, the kiss strove into his mind, how even though they had both been covered in mud, blood and grime, they had shared that special moment which appeared to create this natural valley. He remembered how he wanted to continue the kiss, how he wanted to make her feel precious and special and most of all, out of anything else in the world, loved.

"Earth to Fiero," Jared cut in, gently knocking the dark-haired head with his fist. "Have you even been listening to a word that I've been saying?"

Looking straight up at Jared, not even flinching at the fact that he had been hit repeatedly on the head, the young man smiled dreamily. "I love her, Jared, I love her with all my heart."

Blinking his dark eyes, the other sighed long and hard. "To tell you the truth, Fiero, it was pretty damn obvious." He chuckled a little at the other's stubborn expression before shaking his head. "Trust me, I've seen what happens after a wolf finds their true mate and you most certainly have. But a word of caution." He raised one finger up in-between them., "Don't expect her to jump straight into the same boat as you. She's not the same as us, she hasn't been brought up the way we have. She may initially reject you."

"I know that." Fiero sighed, shaking his head. "Can you imagine what would happen if a total stranger walked up to you and said 'I love you with all my heart and I will never leave your side ever again'?"

"Yeah that would pretty much freak me out," Jared said, rising at the same time as his younger cousin to a standing position. "But something tells me that you two are more aware of one another than you know. Just do me a favour and don't screw up, she's precious that girl and one wrong move could mean that we... sorry you... lose her forever."

Fiero glanced back at the spring-like place they were standing in. "I won't, I can promise you that."

"How do you know?"

The werewolf smirked. "In the dream, she said I was hers."

Chapter 7

First Meeting

Feeling a little like a naughty cub sneaking back into the den after a long night out in the human village over twenty miles away, Fiero slipped stealthily into the kitchen and grabbed a cookie from one of the many jars that were hidden on the top of the dresser. The sun was only just beginning to set, the day finally drawing to a close and he had escaped the rest of the patrol with Jared for the simple reason that the other couldn't be done looking at his love sick expressions. Pausing to listen carefully to the sounds around the house, Fiero confirmed that most of his family were preoccupied with their own activities and turned to make his way to his bedroom.

"Whoa!" he yelped in surprise, colliding with a small-framed body that was topped with black hair. "What are you..."

His words completely failed him as a pair of amber eyes met his and a shockwave of familiarity and fear ran through his entire body. Ekata was staring at him with that nervous little expression of hers and he didn't know whether he should be running or throwing his arms around the girl. "Erm... sorry," he said pathetically, lowering his head a little and rubbing at the top of his spine with his long fingers. "Should've been looking where I was going."

"You're taller," Ekata said softly, blinking up at him, almost as if she were in some form of dream.

He raised an eyebrow at her. "What?"

Gently the girl shook her head. "Sorry, you're taller than you seemed before. Or I'm smaller than I thought..." Idly she flustered, her hands wrangling back and forth across each other. "I don't know what I thought."

Tilting his head to the side, Fiero took in the girl's finer details and compared them to the dream version. Her build was slighter, much more fragile and her pale skin looked like fine porcelain in the fading light. It contrasted with her glistening dark hair and made her strange eyes shine all the more earnestly. An easy smile came to his features as he stepped incredibly close to her, so close in fact that he could feel the heat from the flush that seemed to reverberate throughout her whole body. Ekata was right, she was smaller than before, the tips of her ears only just about reaching his shoulder blades but he was sure that she would have no problems hearing his heartbeat right now. "I like you small, it suits you better," he said, voice quiet and soft, trying not to frighten her away whilst his fingers gently stroked the side of her face.

Ekata tilted her head up to him, fear in her eyes but more out of an unknown sort of feeling he thought than actually being scared of him per se. She took in his height and his width, a usual strong build for a werewolf but there was a grace and a sleekness to Fiero that was different from most wolves. He looked more streamlined, if that made any sense to anyone, like his inner wolf was completely part of him, rather than a separate entity. Even though he was wearing a loose-fitting shirt, she could still see the scars which had been caused to his body all those years ago and she felt a stab of fear go through her heart. "No, we shouldn't." Her voice was a whisper and gently she shook her head, catching his hand. "This is too dangerous."

"No, it's not, Ekata," Fiero said gently, lightly tightening the grip on the hand that held his own and ignoring the slight step back she did at hearing her name. "I'm here for you now. Nothing is going to change that. I can prove it to you as well."

Slowly, her head tilted back up and those strange eyes of amber stared at him levelly. She wasn't going to be fooled again, clearly someone had hurt her in the past and Fiero felt a flare of anger at such a thought. How dare anyone trick and hurt her, regardless of the reason why. Mentally he calmed himself down, he needed to gain her trust and prove to her that he wasn't lying. Taking a deep breath, he closed his eyes and felt the sting coursing through the underside of his lids but only for a few seconds. Once the sensation had stopped, Fiero slowly and carefully opened his usually grey eyes to reveal the striking silver that they had become.

Letting out a gasp of a breath, Ekata found herself moving closer towards the male werewolf without even realizing what she was doing. Her free hand was on his cheek and for a second her lips ghosted over his, a blush on her cheeks. She was virtually on her tiptoes in order to do so but there was still that natural inbuilt fear which stopped her from accepting things at face value. "Fiero?"

"My lady," he replied with a playful little smirk, running his fingers through her thick black hair to tickle at her white ears.

All resistance and fear was suddenly gone from the young Volf and her lips found his all too readily with a hunger that she had never felt before. She felt his arms wrap around her in a tight embrace, providing her with strength and the ability to stand just a little easier. Slowly they broke off from one another, sharing in heavy breaths as they desperately fought to gain air back into their lungs. Feeling the girl move into a much more natural position against him, the wolf gently moved his fingers into the long locks of her hair and stroked them finely. "It's good to find you at long last."

"What's going on?" Ekata asked, a tiny bit of fear in her voice. "I've... I've never..."

Gently Fiero kissed the top of her head. "Don't worry, I'm new to this to."

"But I don't know you." Part of her soul was quite shocked at that statement but the Volf chose to ignore it for now. "I only just met you. Why do I?"

Fiero chuckled. "You really have no idea how to be a wolf do you?"

Ekata blinked. "Should I?"

A racy smile was sent her way in reply, something that set her heart beating just a little faster. "Do you want to learn?" His tone was certainly suggestive but somehow the girl knew that he was to be trusted completely and wouldn't do anything against her will either. How was still something of a mystery but a thrill of emotion crept through her heart and she knew that there was no way that she could refuse him either. Silently she nodded, her eyes glimmering all the more when his smile became just a little more teasing and gently he stepped away, taking her hand and leading her towards the back of the den.

Fiero led her along the passageways, ignoring any of the other members of his family, all his senses and emotions focused only on the girl who was holding onto his hands. There was nothing else in the world that mattered right now, nothing else that meant more to him and he almost felt as though his heart was going to burst. Reaching the back door, Fiero led Ekata out into what could be considered to be the back garden and pulled her to a stop before leaning down to press his lips to hers once again. "Do you trust me?" he asked softly, his large hands resting lightly on her shoulders.

Ekata blinked up at him, quietly biting her lip but nodding softly all the same. She had no idea what was going to happen next but she knew that every fiber of her body was happy to go along with whatever Fiero wanted to do because she was safe with him. It was impossible to explain as to how she knew; she really didn't know anything about the wolf culture in the slightest but for now she would just have to follow her instincts. It didn't stop her flushing bright red when Fiero stepped back and removed his shirt in full view, followed swiftly by his trousers too so that he was standing completely naked in front of her.

Flushing even redder, Ekata wanted to hide her face with her fingers and not look whilst another side of her wanted to leap upon that body and worship it for all that it was worth and another part of her was just perfectly content to stare at him. Gently she gulped, forcing her hands down to her side as she raised her head to look at the wolf in front of her. "Why am I not scared of you?"

"Because you know that I will not hurt you willingly," Fiero said stepping closer. "You know instinctively that we are meant to be one and that in nature we are being nothing but what we are meant to be, Ekata." His fingers found the straps of her dress whilst her nimble and light fingers softly rolled along his abs and up his chest with a fascination of someone who had not touched another before.

A tiny squeak of surprise escaped her as the material of the dress fell away and she tried desperately to cover her own naked body because she was sure that she was nothing worth looking at in the slightest. However, she found her hands splaying flat against the toned abs of her mate – whoa, did that thought really just go through her mind? – as he pressed closer to her with a soft press of a kiss against her forehead. "You have nothing to fear, you outshine the sun and the moon, my love."

Looking up again, Ekata forgot all of her previous nerves and brought her thin arms around the young man's neck, crashing their lips together desperately. Suddenly only senses existed, nothing else lingered around and despite a sharp pang of pain which shot through her body as the wolf within her leapt forth, changing her physically from one form to another which had never been fully released before. Fiero was right beside her, his wolf instinctively warm, protective and prepared to be patient but ready to play.

A swift bop on the nose came from a paw and the next thing either of the young cubs knew they were out, running in the wilderness, free from concerns and worries, being wild and free.

Leaning against the doorframe, Stefina put out a restricting hand towards her mate who had moved as if he were going to go after the pair. "Let them play, Rosario, there's nothing that you can do about this."

"I was going to grab a cup of coffee actually, my love." Rosario smiled towards his mate. "I just hope that he does remember that she is not entirely a wolf. Those defenses are pretty nasty and if he's not careful..."

Stefina let out a half-breathy laugh. "Well, as long as he doesn't do what a certain young cub I know did on his first run with his mate then I'm sure they will be fine."

Lightly pushing his glasses up his nose, the wolf sighed. "You're still never going to let me live that down are you?"

"What do you think?" Stefina raised her eyebrows slightly, before moving to a calendar on the wall and marking the date. Feeling the silent question, she sighed. "Just marking the first run, I doubt either of them will pay attention enough to remember it."

Hearing the kettle click, Rosario turned around and set about doing what he had planned on doing all along. Gently his eyes drifted to one of the numerous family photographs, this one of his departed sister with a very small cub that eventually grew into Fiero in her arms. Blinking, he shook his head, wondering why he ever doubted himself over the whole situation, it was easy to see even then, Fiero's mother had known that her son would go on and be something extraordinarily special.

Chapter 8

A Stab in the Dark

The scent was alluring, which immediately put Jared onto more of an edge than anything else had previously done. There was rarely a time when a scent the likes of which he was tracking now led to anything good and he knew almost automatically that trouble would just be around the corner. It didn't stop him blinking as he entered a natural clearing and spotted a lithe female figure with a long mane of shocking red hair, just simply standing there. The scent was stronger now, for a weaker being it would have brought them straight to the female but the young werewolf just smirked. "Very pretty, I must admit. But you're going to have to try harder than that, vampire, to allure me to your bedside."

For a second the figure didn't react, then slowly turned her head in almost a childish manner as if she were hiding some great secret from the world. "Oh, I wouldn't need to allure you to get you to my bedside." She turned, dropping her arms slowly to reveal what Jared expected. "I think you like what you see?"

Gently, the werewolf leaned against the nearest oak tree available. "Like I said before, very pretty. Especially nice touch on using your hair to hide the bits that most men would want to see. But like I said before, you are going to have to try harder than that, *vampire.*" There was no disguising the venom in his voice and his eyes glimmered with the potential thrill of the upcoming fight. "Because I am a wolf and could tear you apart without even thinking about it."

Siren smiled, hardly seeming fazed by this information. "Yet you treat the one who is neither of us like a sister, curious."

"I have no idea what you are talking about." Jared pushed himself off the tree to stare levelly at the girl. "And I suggest you get off our territory before I dispense with the-"

Suddenly the red-haired vampire was right in front of his face, that beautiful white skin merely centimeters from his own. Instincts kicked in and he lashed out at the girl, claws painfully forming through his human skin. He just missed as the vampire pulled herself back out of his grasp and Jared wondered for a brief second as to why she had even pulled the move in the first place.

There was a sudden pain from his midriff and blood welled up in his mouth. Glancing down he could just see the hilt of a dagger, laced with gold and silver and painfully he slumped down towards the ground. Siren leered over him, her eyes glistening brightly. "You should have taken the opportunity to be allured, it would have been less painful way for you to die."

The vampire laughed, loud and cruel and stepped away from the suffering werewolf who mentally cursed his own stupidity. "Don't worry, I'll make sure that the girl gets everything that she deserves. I'm sure her freshly spilt blood will make a fine trophy for my brother."

It was getting darker for Jared, the world around him becoming cold and filled with nothing but an empty void. One thought stuck in his head though, one over-riding notion that he couldn't allow the festering she-devil who had managed to get through the first wave of vampire defenses any further than she had come. Half-aware of what was going on around him; the eldest cub glanced up at the tree and spotted an age-old symbol carved deep into the wood. It was probably the longest of long shots for him to take but the silver in the dagger was so close to consuming him that he would take any shot that presented itself.

With a growl to rival the ancient battles of old, the young werewolf propelled himself upwards and slammed his bloodied hand onto the marking. His vision blacked out but he still heard the high-pitch wail of the vampire as the ancient magic reacted to her. "Should've taken the opportunity to kill me outright," he muttered with a twisted smile to himself before collapsing into the snow, his blood mingling with the frozen water around him almost as if to permanently mark it as his final resting place. His last thoughts, before the darkness hit him, were that he should warn Fiero about the vampire's presence but the darkness just willingly took him instead.

~ ~

Coming to a panting stop, Ekata felt all of her legs virtually give way under her and flopped down into the snow below for some kind of rest. She couldn't even recall the last time that she had been in this form, let alone tried to run after anyone in it. Fiero seemed to be perfectly happy just lolling about in his wolf form, but he had grown up knowing the inner beast and had no problems adapting to it. Ekata on the other hand had been aware but had never really changed into the stark white wolf that she currently was, and whilst natural instinct kicked in for the most part and made her move and at least act a little wolfish, running for such a long time made her feel more exhausted than depriving herself of blood.

She remained where she was for a moment, heaving out huge clouds of steamy breath before twisting her head suddenly towards the very distant horizon. Just on the very edge of her vision, where a darkened line of mountains broke the definition between sky and ground, there was a sudden bolt of white light that seemed to almost reach up to the heavens itself. Amber eyes tracked a fine pulse that rose up the beam of light and for a second, she thought that it was going to drop straight down again but instead she realised that it had moved several miles to the west of the first light location. "Dymas?" she whispered silently, feeling the air around her heat up briefly for a second or two. "You need to come here... bring him here..."

For a moment there may have been the start of a second flash, there was plenty of static around her fur and for the smallest second of time she felt a connection being made. But then it was robbed away, someone at the other end had latched onto the caster and the chance was gone. A soft snow flurry landed on her white fur and Ekata glanced up at the sky. "What am I doing?"

"Hey." Fiero's voice came softly from the side and a large black wolf with white highlights and those stunning silver eyes approached her. "I didn't go too fast for you did I?"

Ekata paused and thought for a moment. "You did actually." But her attention turned back to the distant horizon. "Though if you hadn't then I wouldn't have seen..."

"Your brother?"

"How do you know about that?"

Fiero fidgeted with his paws. "It was something my mother told me once. An ancient story about a Silver Maiden and her brother..."

"We are not them," Ekata said carefully, trying to look away but finding that it merely confused her vision somewhat. "Everyone seems to think we are, but we are not."

Gently the black wolf stepped up to the glistening white one and nuzzled into the side of her neck. "Do you really believe that?"

"It's the one thing that has kept me alive all these years," Ekata replied as she stood up and took a step to the side but instead collapsed back towards the ground.

With reflexes that defied every known law of motion, Fiero carefully guided his mate back down to a lying position. "If it's too tiring you can change back you know; I won't get offended."

There was a worried look from those amber eyes, "But—"

Sensing her discomfort, Fiero allowed himself to change back into his human form though he would have preferred to remain in wolf form. The winter wasn't as cold as it was to humans but bare flesh did tend to have some sensitive areas. The white wolf looked unsettled for a few seconds, almost prepared to bolt away from him but gently he placed his hand upon her head and stroked through the silken fur gently. *I'm not going to make you do anything that you don't want to do, my dear Ekata, I merely want you to be happy and free.*

Looking back out towards the horizon, Ekata wondered if she dare before giving in to some inner feeling which she just didn't understand right now or would fully focus on. It was quite painful turning back, feeling her bones and muscles realign themselves with a series of crunches and clicks and tears of pain came to her eyes once the transformation was complete. She let out a few mewls of withheld pain as she felt Fiero lean down and kiss away the tears that were welling in her amber eyes. "Don't hold back, I won't think any less of you for such things."

But Ekata did hold back because she knew that if she started weeping over the pain that was going through her body right now, then she would never actually stop crying. It was like every last bone in her body was on fire and the slightest move would break her into a thousand pieces. She felt the other's smile, "Stubborn cub." The whisper from the male was soft and gentle; "You don't have to hide... not anymore."

"Why do you talk like you know me?"

Fiero smiled. "When did we first meet?"

"The other night, by the river... you had fallen down the bank side and..." She sighed and looked away, knowing what he was trying to say. "That was a dream. I don't know you and I can't just trust you... you don't know what it's like to be hated, hunted all of your life just because you could be something to someone who doesn't care about you in the slightest."

For a few seconds there was a lingering silence between the pair and slowly amber eyes rose to meet the silver. "Why do I even care about you?"

Their lips met again, this time a feeling of warmth going through her body which drove out the ice-cold sting of the snow where it was allowed to touch her bare skin as Fiero had her carefully wrapped around his large and warm body. Ekata's mind was filled with nothing but thoughts of comfort, of a strength that she had never felt and most of all, an alien emotion of love. Briefly she saw an image of a house and children running around, but most of all, Fiero striding home with a fresh catch and that daredevil smile which always made her heart melt.

"I may not understand what you've been through, but I did see it and I was there. If it is within my ability, I'll ensure that no one can ever hurt you ever again." The words ghosted over her lips and slowly she found herself rising into a kneeling position, whilst Fiero's hands ran smoothly down her sides, encouraging but not demanding. Patient and pliant, soft and gentle yet strong and determined and knowing exactly what to do.

Those silver eyes however remained fixed on her amber ones. Slowly she took hold of his hand. "Do you know what you are getting yourself into, Fiero?"

"No." There was that smirk again, melting her heart and making everything seem wonderfully hazy, but also in very sharp focus. Fiero lightly blinked and let his fingers run through her hair once again, enjoying the rich texture. "But all I do know is that you are my mate and even if I have to go to the depths of hell and back then I'll do it for you. I'll always come for you; I'll always find you and bring back that smile to your face."

Ekata leaned forward, her heart beating rapidly but in a way which felt good. "Then turn me into a wolf, make me no longer be a Volf."

Chapter 9

Talk of Silver

There was a slight crash, followed by several thumps and a distinct muttering of curses that alerted Disreli to the fact that Rosario had entered his personal room. Not that he needed any sounds to do that of course, he could smell the wolf he still considered to be a cub a good distance away. "If you're going to wreck my place," he chided lightly, "at least let me know in advance."

Sitting in his big leather high-backed chair, Disreli looked old and very worn out. His skin was rough, years upon years of hard work showing through in a variety of liver spots and age-old scars which had next to no meaning now. His fingers were long and spindly, almost devoid of muscles and appearing to be mere bones covered by flaking skin. His hair was long and grey, though there was no beard present as Disreli still insisted in shaving with a cut-throat razor. However, it was easy to call Disreli wolfish in appearance, something about his stance and the positioning of his facial features gave off that impression and the piercing blue eyes spoke of age and wisdom but a sharp alertness that defied the outer appearance. Plus, being surrounded by a whole host of leather books and boxes most definitely added to the impression.

"You know you really should let Stefina in here one day to tidy up or organise," Rosario easily chided back towards his eldest brother. "Then I wouldn't end up destroying the place every time I come in here."

"Hello, Ro-ro," was the only reply that he got from Disreli, jesting to his youngest brother, as he would forever tease him with the name that the wolf before him had first called himself from the first time he could speak. "I am glad you came as early as you could. I believe my time is beginning to run short on this world."

"Don't say that," Rosario said, having heard that statement one too many times from the older wolf as he pulled up a seat in front of him. "The only day you will run short is when you misjudge a hill for a cliff."

Disreli chuckled, deeply and with humour. "Ah, I see you still remember much and haven't gone soft. A trait which you have successfully passed onto all of your sons... and our nephew."

"Fiero? That cub is more forgetful than a goldfish." The tone was deadpan but affectionately so. "Though I raised him no different than the others. Once he gets his head screwed on I'm sure that he'll be a fine young wolf."

"His head has already been screwed on and it won't leave him anytime soon." Disreli smiled. "Not even on his first run with his newly acquired mate."

There was no need for surprise; the things that this ancient wolf knew were enough to boggle the mind of even the greatest of seers throughout the world. Plus, anyone could have heard Jared's story and taken a pretty good guess at what would happen if they knew about ancient wolf lore. "That is good to know, she is one very special young lady and I would hate to think what would happen if he were ever to hurt or lose her."

"Something which unfortunately has to happen in this turn of events." The comment was sad, lonely and almost spoken without any real thought but Disreli shifted and pushed forward a strange-looking box which he must have been fiddling with at some point during the last few days. It looked like some form of oak musical box, the ones with the little spinning ballerinas in and it smelt old. "But I want you to take this and see if it can possibly bring about an end."

"An end to what?" Rosario carefully took the box away from the delicate fingers, feeling his curiosity spiked despite the inevitable confusion that he was about to go through.

"The world, life itself... maybe even the whole of creation." Disreli sighed. "But within, may be the key to salvation and renewal."

For a second, Rosario frowned at the other but then focused his attention on the box. It was plainly decorated, oak having a quality all of its own regardless of what others may think of it and there were no obvious traps or trick locks. Carefully he opened it, and saw only two things. A small mirror mounted into the inner section of the lid and a small, plain-looking red leather book. Picking it up, he flipped it around a few times and found himself harking back to the days when his older brother would test him by placing some magic artifact in front of him to see what the cub would do with it.

Quietly, Disreli watched his younger brother, noting how age was only just starting to settle on the youngster's shoulders. Even though he knew that the other was an alpha now, with a beautiful wife and a whole host of children he could still see the young man with the dark hair who had defied his wishes all those years ago and struck out to become a Hunter. In some respects, Rosario had made the bravest decision and proven himself to be just what the world needed but the elder sometimes wondered what would have happened if he had remained at home like he had requested.

There came the sounds of paper being flicked through, which distracted Disreli from those thoughts. "This is Cresta Du Winter's diary... from before she had Ekata?" Rosario's voice had a note of concern in it.

"The lead-up to it, I believe," Disreli said gently. "But it is only part of the picture. She believed that she had destroyed it upon the birth of the twins but it merely slipped through the hands of fate into my lap and has remained with me ever since."

Rosario paused, half-reading a paragraph of the finely sculpted text and glanced up. "How? Is that where you were stationed?"

Disreli nodded slightly, his blue eyes turning back to the roaring fire and took the heat in for a few long seconds. "Like I said, she believed that she had destroyed it upon the birth of the twins... she asked for it to be destroyed as she wanted no one to know her thoughts throughout everything."

"She gave you it?"

"No, someone else did."

For a second, Rosario wondered if he would get a straight answer out of Disreli if he asked the obvious question, and decided to chance it anyway. "Who?"

"One of her servants," Disreli said, shifting a little uncomfortably. "I never quite got the name unfortunately. All I was told was that my lady wished me to destroy the diary and never repeat anything that was written in it to another soul. I've kept the second part of that request until today."

The younger wolf with the lighter grey hair didn't reply for a few seconds, he had opened a random page in the diary and was speed reading the text. His face paled for a second and he re-read a passage more slowly this time. "Disreli... please tell me that you are not that girl's father."

A snort of a laugh escaped him. "Whatever gives you that impression."

"Disreli, my manservant gave me comfort tonight. A beautiful man of body and heart..." Reading aloud, Rosario cast his eyes towards his brother, praying silently that he was completely reading the situation wrong.

For once, the old man managed to look a little on the bashful side. "I believe that was a good thirty years before the birth of the twins. I got into a lot of trouble for that, from all fronts I can assure you."

"Twins." Rosario frowned slightly, his thoughts jumping far ahead of the situation as they were apt to do when he was thinking. "I thought they were supposed to be brother and sister?"

"That's what non-fraternal twins are, Rosario."

Slowly a sigh was repressed. "I didn't mean it like that. From all my readings of the Silver Maiden and Golden Prince, they are never described as being twins. They're always brother and sister, one older and one younger..." His eyes cast back down to the diary and he flicked the last entry and then the first. "If they are who they are reputed to be, why are they twins all of a sudden?"

Disreli smiled. "Because this world we live in is a renewal to try and correct something that went wrong before."

Slowly the alpha of the pack cast his eyes up to his elder brother. "Excuse me?"

"There are those of a certain school of thought that believe this world is merely a replacement for another one, almost like an alternative timeline to a series of events. The only thing that remains constant within the world is the legend of the Silver and the Gold." Disreli licked his lips slowly. "You don't believe a word of it, do you?"

For a few seconds the younger werewolf considered his response. "If that were so, then surely there would have to be someone who knew what the world was like before this one replaced it. Whilst there are some who are crazy enough to believe..." Rosario blinked and stared down at the Diary once again. "He wouldn't have allowed his son to not know about it."

A crinkled old smile crossed the face. "That is why I always liked you best, Rosario, you always think outside the box."

"Hardly." Rosario smiled back. "I just read people very well and I know that Amaranth would have told Fiero something from the start. Even if he were too young to really understand it. Plus, Genii wasn't one to hide her visions from her children either... yet, Fiero doesn't know much about what he is supposed to be. If this is an alternative world to fix something that has been mistakenly done..."

Blinking, Rosario paused and looked down at the book, trying to work out just at what point this conversation had gotten completely crazy and realised that his elder brother was probably tormenting him with mind tricks again. In the past it had been one of the few things that really drove him to distraction but the older werewolf now lived in a world where anything and everything could happen. "You know something about this, don't you, Disreli?" he questioned carefully. "And you may have just told me all about it... but you've masked it from my mind right?"

Disreli nodded slowly. "Yes until the time is right for you to be gifted with the knowledge. Because there is nothing to be done about what is to play out. If I could still trap you within the realm of confused and fluctuating thoughts as easily as I used to when you were a cub, then I would not have to face this unpleasant situation."

"If you're talking about the two vampires on our land." Rosario flicked his fingers across his face just to make sure that he wasn't jumping again and realised irritatingly that he probably was. "I know about them already and have increased the—"

"Jared's dead." The reply was flat and devoid of emotion. "What?"

Disreli sighed. "Michael's at the door..."

Without so much as a pause, Rosario was up and out of the chair and quickly disappeared from the room. He left the diary behind but Disreli knew that the other would come back for it. For a moment or two he sighed, staring into the roaring flames and listening to the emptiness of the space around him. "I wouldn't recommend trying to drink from that goblet, it's poison to vampires like you."

"I didn't come here to drink." The voice was tired, filled with excess air and seemed to be almost frustrated beyond the point of no return. "Why do you insist...you know what he'll do..."

"You can't interfere, boy," Disreli said gently, his eyes remaining firmly on the flames. "This has to play out."

"He'll kill her." The tone was more desperate now, more pressing. Clearly the black-haired vampire was starting to come around from the drugs which had been given to him. "You know what he'll do to her..."

The wolf sighed. "You should be resting; you will need to regain your strength."

"Let me go, old man, and I'll show you what strength I have." there was no real threat behind the voice, it was merely the sound of a very desperate man trying to reach out to the last thing that was blocking his current path.

Disreli shook his head. "Not until the Blood Moon rises. I made my promise and I will abide by my oath. Go back to sleep for a while, you'll feel much better when you awake... Raphael." For a fraction of a second there was a yell of defiance but it got cut off abruptly, followed by a slight thunk.

The werewolf waited patiently for a few seconds before pulling himself out of the chair and turning to look. In the farthest corner of the room, slumped across a table was a pale-skinned vampire with midnight-black hair and an ancient-looking but still highly regarded black Templar uniform. His grey eyes were closed in enforced sleep and his eyelids fluttered with movement as dreams kept him under the dangerously soft spell. Just though, Raphael played down his powers but he was immensely strong.

For a second, Disreli felt like reaching out and touching the boy's hair, just to give him some inner comfort or reason to be in this situation but knew that the slightest touch would wake him from slumber. Gently he sighed, shaking his head. "You're playing a very dangerous game, Alcarde, and to risk your own life is one thing but to risk your children's is another. I will keep my promise though, until my last breath..." carefully he cast his blazing blue eyes up to the ceiling though appeared to be seeing beyond it. "But it must come soon, else all will be lost once again."

Chapter 10

Plotting and Planning

"You know, you really didn't need to kill that werewolf," Mephistopheles said, almost idly staring towards the fire which he had set up whilst Siren had been out on her little patrol. "He would have made a good font of knowledge about this place and some of its hidden traps."

There was a seething silence from the girl sitting on the opposite side of the fire, glowering at the flames which continued to dance back and forth despite her attempts to put them out. Most vampires feared fire, it was one of the few things that they could be honestly attributed with in all of human mythology, but for Mephistopheles it was nothing short of a route to power. To be able to withstand the sight of the roaring flames and barely bat an eyelid at them made for a creation of a bigger threat than he really was. Not that he wasn't a threat of course, to most younger vampires he was held as the pinnacle of personal achievement and advancement, the elders regarded him with disdain and distrust but would make no move to stop his actions. They knew a potential successor when they saw one.

Of course, that would naturally be after he had successfully claimed the powers of creation and destruction from the twins. A secret he guarded so close to his heart that it got mobbed over by many other thoughts and became hard to find. Everyone thought that he was just acting on the advice of his mother, if truth be told Mephistopheles wanted nothing more than to steal all of the power for himself. That way he would be complete and would be able to wipe out the mistakes he had made in the past.

Erase the one thing that stood in his way, that obstacle that had been present in his life far too long. Even before he was born it had been there and he hated it all the more for that very reason. But he pushed those thoughts aside, even though Siren was insane as they came and currently seething from the pain she was undoubtedly going through due to the ancient spell which had attacked her, she did still have some form of mind to think things through occasionally and lingering on his own personal matters would do him no good right now.

"Really you should have brought him back here so that we could have tortured him a little," he said cruelly, picking a small amount of grit from in-between his teeth and flicked it away. "It would have been a good game for you at the very least."

"He didn't even yield to the seduction," Siren said slowly, her eyes still fixed on the fire. "He wouldn't have given up anything to us." Her voice was mature, firm and well spoken, more like a deadly vampire lady than the insane creature she was normally. Gently she shook out her auburn hair. "He was trained, unknowingly. He would have been useless to us."

"What makes you so certain, sister?" Mephistopheles said smarmily, not liking this side of Siren in the slightest as he never truly knew how to react to her. "Anyone will break under our torture regime; it's all a matter of finding the right button to press. Werewolves are especially easy to mess with because they're family orientated. All it takes is a simple slip and they all go down together."

There was silence for a few long seconds from the female vampire, before her strange eyes slowly rose to stare levelly at his light grey ones. "At least they remain a family..." her words lingered for a few seconds then she turned her attention away to something else that caught her eye, "and don't take advantage for their own personal gain."

For a second Mephistopheles felt a stirring of change and automatically lowered his hand to the hidden dagger in his waistband. He knew full well what the female was referring to but didn't want to act overly rashly. This was the most dangerous that Siren could ever be and if he played the game wrong then everything he had worked for would be all for naught.

However, Siren merely returned to looking at the flames for a few seconds before skulking back to hide away in the approaching shadows which she must have called forth. She didn't speak another word and clearly opted to take rest and recover from everything that she had gone through.

Mephistopheles let out a slow breath, one he had only just been aware of holding and let go of the hidden blade. "At least you're easier to control than that idiotic brother of ours, Siren, that little twerp would have figured out what I was up to ages ago even though he's as thick as two short planks."

Shaking his head, he rose to a standing position and moved away from the fire, extinguishing it with a wave of his hand. He still had to figure out how to get past the defenses and also a way to infiltrate the very strongly bound pack but he felt at least a little confident now that there were at least a few places where the defenses were weaker. Briefly he headed to the place where the werewolf had been slain but knew that it would be next to impossible to pass that way again without alerting the pack that he was around. Blood was a very dangerous component in any type of magic and even in the quick way that it had been haphazardly used, the effect would be something extraordinary to behold.

Reaching a crossroads in the path he was following, the vampire paused for a few seconds before opting to take the longer road which appeared to swerve off into the distant tree line of a nearby forest. The other two pathways appeared to lead back towards the pack Den and he did not like the idea of coming face to face with a grieving wolf pack. He could just about recall the pack that used to guard his family and how they had gone crazy upon the death of one of their lower members.

Slowly he made his way down the previously unexplored path and Mephistopheles found himself wandering slightly away from the forest where he had presumed that it would take him and into the wide open fields that were usually hidden from human view. There was a slight incline to his steps, suggesting that this was the start of a hill or a mountain.

Vaguely the vampire frowned, wondering why the wolves would choose such a place when he just caught the sound of something approaching. Quickly the tall vampire pulled himself back into the shadows and masked his presence as best as he could. Though he did just briefly take note that the defenses here were next to none existent, before the cold grey eyes focused in almost directly on a pure white wolf which had literally just stepped cautiously down into the clearing and was sniffing the air as if it were aware of something being amiss.

The creature looked starkly beautiful, highlighting the snow around it; the fur seeming to shimmer gently in the rays of moonlight which were creeping across the expanse of the early night. Even for a creature that would normally be repulsed by the other, Mephistopheles had to reflect silently that the wolf was a prize to behold. A few purposeful strides were taken by the creature and it lowered its black nose to lightly sniff at something the vampire couldn't see. The muscles weren't as defined, suggesting a youngster underneath and a certain fineness which lacked from the usual maddening brood.

For a second the vampire thought that he may have been spotted as the wolf turned to look directly at him, amber eyes boring into the space where he was. Blinking in shock, Mephistopheles felt his jaw virtually drop. That beautiful and prize-worthy-looking wolf was his missing half-bastard sister Ekata?

Surely this had to be some form of trick; she was a repulsive creature and should have looked like a scruffy mongrel. But there was no denying it, those strange eyes were fairly unique and he noted briefly that there was a newer flame in them, something that hadn't been there before. There was still the fear, testament to the years of enforced terror at the hands of their mother but at the same time there was something new. Something he hadn't ever seen before in the midst of those strange orbs.

A will to survive, a purpose for living other than just existing. Was she in love? How was such a thing possible, she was a disgusting Volf a creature made up of a vampire and a werewolf? She was unbalanced, dangerous and impossible to predict for all the wrong reasons. How could anything come to love something so dangerous and monstrous?

The amber eyes blinked once before turning away to focus on a second wolf that appeared. This one was clearly a werewolf, much larger and sleek with tinges of white to define the midnight-black fur. The creature moved towards the female and gently nuzzled against her head, as if checking that everything was okay. The size difference almost made it appear to be a completely different type of relationship if it wasn't for the fact that the fresh scent on both of them was particularly strong. Mephistopheles snarled quietly but then sharply focused on hiding his presence all the more as the male wolf had turned his attention towards the tree line where he was.

The creature's eyes were burning silver, something which was a physical impossibility, or at the very least should have been one. But it was right there in front of him.

So that is the Guardian of the Silver Maiden he thought quietly to himself. *No wonder the old tales speak of a great warning of him. Even though I despise myself for it, I must say you definitely choose well, Ekata. All for naught though, for I will take that little brat down if he dares to attack me right now.*

Mephistopheles noticed that Ekata had hunkered down in the snow a little, the male wolf stepping around her and beginning to bare his large white teeth. A smirk crossed the vampires features, hand slipping down towards the dagger which was just at his side and he prepared for the fight which was brewing. The thrill of it, the taste of two adversaries facing one another. It had been such a long time since he had even had the slightest taste of something that worth his attention and it was only several hundred years of training which stopped him from leaping at the werewolf first and drawing forth that heated blood.

A lone, mournful howl suddenly hit the air and ripped apart the surrounding silence. Even the vampire was surprised by the sound and stepped back further, wanting nothing more than to get out of the way of such a horrible sound. It spoke of sadness, anger and regret and was quickly joined by others, turning it into a wail that echoed back off of every root, trunk and branch in the forest.

The vampire covered his ears as best as he could, feeling the wave of emotions running through his body as if he were being struck by thousands of volts of electricity. Very slowly the sound faded, sweeping down the hill as the message was passed on and Mephistopheles removed his hands.

He wasn't surprised to see small spatters of blood on his skin and was pretty sure that he had bitten his lip enough to draw his own blood as well. Running a hand across his mouth to confirm, the vampire stared grimly to the last place he had seen the two wolves and noted that they were now gone. Only paw prints just about visible in the snow as the heavens above had deemed it a perfect moment to start a new flurry of the frozen water crystals.

"Tch," he commented to himself, glancing around to make sure that there were no more surprises waiting for him before heading back towards the small camp. They would have to move and he would rather deal with a hurting and angry Siren any day of the week than listen to the howls of sadness that were undoubtedly going to fill the air for the rest of the night.

Plus, they had to find somewhere a little safer to hide, even in the middle of winter the sun was lethal in the open areas that they had surrounding them. Grimly he set off, wondering just how he was supposed to deal with this ever-growing situation. "Damn brats, I should have just done the job myself when I first learned the truth. Then I wouldn't be dealing with this mess."

~ ~

Fiero paused only briefly in the doorway, changing back to his human form though he could already feel the sadness and anxiety in the rooms ahead. Ekata was quickly by his side, shaking in fear and there were already trickles of tears falling down her face. Silently he passed her a piece of clothing that was hanging on a peg near the back door, not even bothering to check to see what it was before stepping forth to find out the full extent of the emotional outburst. It didn't matter that he was about to walk stark naked into the room, there were probably a fair few others who were in the same state of dress but he knew that his mate was still a little unused to this whole situation and it would not do to distress her any more than undoubtedly this situation would.

Still he had to smile faintly when he felt her fingers latch lightly onto his own, he could virtually feel her heart beat racing through the delicate touch and lightly he sighed. "Whatever we're about to face in there, Ekata," he whispered quietly to her, "it's not your fault."

"How can you say that, knowing what I am?" Ekata whispered back, sounding more desperate than she had done before. "I should have left as soon as I woke."

Rather than dignifying that statement with an answer, Fiero tightened his grip on the little female and led them into the room. Almost instantly, the stench of blood and death hit him and he wasn't surprised to see virtually all the current pack members joined together in their shared grief. A few of the younger ones glanced up in their direction, but their eyes quickly averted. They were only curious to see who was arriving so late and no questions were brought to them.

Stepping closer, the werewolf felt his heart clench in sudden pain upon seeing Jared lying out on the floor, his body forever trapped in its last form and the dagger protruding from his chest. He didn't need to ask what had happened, none of it mattered. The heir to the pack was dead, killed within his own territory and mercilessly left to the whims of the wood.

Grabbing hold of his mate, he pulled the sobbing girl into his tight and loving embrace and mentally told her to remain silent. Now was not the time for words, they were merely here to share in their grief of the situation. Glancing towards his Uncle Rosario, he saw the old wolf looking lost and strained, almost as if he didn't quite believe that this was happening but there was a distinct edge to the other, something that gave away the perfect meaning of why he was still the alpha after all of these years. The wolf stood over his first son, dark fur rustling back and forth in a silent wind of anger and hatred but it was clear to see that grief was his primary concern right now.

Slowly the dark eyes flicked up towards the pair and narrowed only slightly for a second but more in an acceptance of the fact that right now he didn't want to talk to anyone. Fiero knew that Rosario wouldn't blame Ekata nor would he want her out of the Den anytime soon. Whilst her presence had instigated this whole scenario she had never deliberately set it up and after all his years as a Hunter it would be foolish to lay the blame solely on the girl. The eyes flickered away from the pair though, an almost casual head toss indicating to the younger wolf was to take the girl away from this scene in order to calm down and regain herself. It wasn't a rejection from the pack or anything, just an acceptance that Ekata was an outsider who wouldn't know how to deal with these occurrences.

Silently nodding, Fiero gently picked up his mate and headed out of the room, barely aware that none of the other wolves even paid attention to his departure. Silently he pushed the door closed and debated where next to head, as he knew that he had to calm Ekata down and talk rationally to her but also make her understand that she was still very much loved and wasn't about to be rejected. At least not by him in the grand scheme of life. He took a step towards the room where she was staying before changing his mind and turning back down the long winding corridors to his own room. It was far enough away from the one currently filled with grieving wolves but close enough that if they were needed to be summoned then they could be easily found.

Quietly he opened the door and shut it before moving to lay Ekata on the bed. Before she could even begin to mutter a single word towards him, the werewolf placed his lips on hers in a slow and long passionate kiss. Gently he ran his fingers through her long fine hair but couldn't think of a way to start explaining anything. "Ekata," he murmured quietly, pausing to take a breath of air only to find that the girl returned to the kiss, gently wrapping her arms around his body and pulling him closer. He didn't ask anything more, or try to explain. They both just needed to let themselves be ruled by emotion right at that second in time and neither one was going to deny the other of that attention.

Chapter 11

What must come to pass

The day was nearly over, the moon appearing faintly in the sky above as Ekata stared silently out of the window, amazed that she was even able to stand right now. Whilst she still didn't quite understand what was going on in her head regarding Fiero, her heart and body knew to yield to inner instincts and not to question too much. Never before had she experienced anything like this, not to say that she wasn't entirely innocent as there had been others in the past, potentials who had either slipped from her grasp or else simply faded when she had been forced to move on; but Fiero stood out beyond all of those prior and not just because he was the first werewolf she had ever fallen in love with. Gently her white ears flicked at that thought, love was a very strange emotion.

But her thoughts were clouded by the scent of grief that seeped through every pore in the house. She felt her amber eyes sting once again with tears because she knew that regardless of what was said her presence in the Den was the cause of the heirs' death. If she had never lingered then he would still be alive and enjoying his life. Gently she gripped the windowsill and tried to stop her heart breaking into thousands of pieces.

"You better not be thinking what I know you're thinking." Fiero's voice drifted across before his strong and bold arms wrapped around her body. "You are part of this pack, Ekata, that will not change."

"I am the reason he is dead," the girl spoke, trying to keep her voice as strong as possible despite the fact she was shivering like crazy. "Nothing that either of us can say will ever change that fact. If I wasn't here..."

Fiero sighed. "They would have you captured and tortured for something that you may possibly become. Ekata, I know you don't want to hear this now but you are not solely responsible for what happened. You didn't drive that dagger into his heart; you didn't send him out on that patrol. He knew the dangers of facing vampires alone... he made his own choice."

"How can you not hate me? He was your brother." Ekata nearly shrieked as tears began to fall from her eyes. "Wherever I go I bring nothing but destruction and despair. When does it stop, Fiero? When everyone that you know and love is dead?"

Gently the werewolf ran his fingers through his mate's hair, forcing her to look up at him once again before placing his lips onto hers. This time it was gentle and inquisitive, like a child taking his first steps into the world. "Do you want me to hate you?" he asked, his voice low and tender.

Ekata shook her head, pulling herself against his strong body. "Of course I don't. But..."

"Listen to me, and listen well." His voice was firmer now, it held a note of authority and justice about it.

"Regardless of what you have been told in the past, you are not to blame for this present moment. If anyone is, it's me. I should have let you go on that night; I should have stayed indoors and let you run blindly free. If I had ignored the strange feeling in my soul, then this wouldn't have happened in the slightest." Gently, he pushed the fragile-looking girl back from him. "But if I had ignored it, then I would have never met you either. I would have never felt anything like this and that is something too precious for me to let go of now."

Staring at him strangely, the Volf blinked her amber eyes at him almost as if she didn't understand what he was saying. But a tiny fragment of a smile crossed her lips and her fingers were lightly on the side of his face without any trouble. "What happens if I turn on you? What happens when the blood moon rises and I become a vampire... will you still love me even if I tear out your heart and eat it?"

"You wouldn't do that." The smirk reflected in his voice and his eyes flashed silver. "By the time that happens, I hope you'll be pregnant with the start of our own pack."

Ekata visibly flinched away from him, blinking in confusion. "Excuse me?"

Fiero frowned at the girl. "You seriously don't expect that?"

"But I... I can't..." She looked visibly flustered by the suggestion and also floored that Fiero would think of such a thing. Though she had to admit that it was a perfect distraction to her current mood. "I don't... I mean. I'm not built... like other women."

"Other women?"

Ekata looked away. "I can't bear children. I don't have anything down there; it was taken away when I was a child..."

Still looking bewildered for a few seconds, Fiero suddenly chuckled and shook his head. "Oh, my dearest, Ekata, you really don't know much about being a werewolf do you?"

"Huh?"

Fiero gently shook his head. "Now is not the time but when the grieving is done, it may be wise for you to speak to my aunt and my female cousins. Because regardless of what you have been told, one day we will have cubs of our own. That I can promise you."

Staring at her - she tried to select the right terminology for what Fiero was to her now but failed as her mind just went around in circles – she tried to think of the possibility of having children with Fiero. Her mind's eye flickered, imaging what a family with Fiero would look like and she found her lips on his again as joy surged through her.

For a second she felt light and wonderful and so free of all the madness but then another howl cut through the growing darkness, this time it could only belong to Disreli and the sadness refilled her. The kiss broke naturally between them and she rested her head against his chest, listening to his heart beat and allowed herself to fall into the same pattern as the rest of the pack.

~ ~ ~

There were virtually no words spoken as Jared's body was carried to the funeral pyre, wrapped in the blanket that he had held onto since he was a cub and his features appearing to be so serene and peaceful. Almost as if all the pain and anguish had left him. He was supported on a wooden bed that was carried by four wolves, though if truth be told two could have probably managed it. Rosario stood next to the pyre, watching as his son was lowered down with reverence and respect. The wind whipped at the long cloak which he wore, his human flesh barely noting the stinging cold from the ice snow which continued to fall in flurries all around them. Every single member of the pack was in human form, similarly decked out in the long black cloaks, each in their respective places. Excluding Fiero who now stood off to the side from his cousins, his mate next to him, whereas in the past he would have stood shoulder to shoulder with them. He hadn't been rejected, he had been given new responsibilities and soon would break off from the main family pack to form his own with Ekata.

No words were spoken; no howls filled the air, just the silence of the snow falling and the occasional caw of a hidden raven in the darkness of the woods. Stefina approached, baring a flaming torch and flanked by her daughters who carried oil-stained rags. Slowly they moved past their mother, careful to not allow any of the embers to touch the precious burdens they carried before laying them around their fallen brother in a set pattern, the last being folded out to fully cover the body.

Ekata watched with horrified fascination as Stefina stepped forward and placed the flaming torch against the nearest rag. It burst into flames which then spread to the others quickly in succession before roaring over the body and sinking into the wood and moss below. It was only at that moment that she realised that each of the rags represented each of the immediate family members of the wolf who had fallen and she felt fresh tears pool into her eyes.

However, something stirred within her, a calmness which she had never felt before and unconsciously she shifted her stance. The forest around her became a wash of noise as the birds chirped back and forth to one another, the insects scurried about and the wind whistled through the ancient bark. The river where she had met Fiero babbled over the stones and the delicate white flowers which had appeared seemed to rustle in a breeze that brought out their natural fragrance swirling back towards the pyre. Raising her head, her hood falling away as she did so, Ekata stared directly at the flames which rose high into the darkening sky. Everyone else present had their heads bowed in respect and memory.

"Eldora," she whispered, feeling the wind respond to her as well as a faint stinging in her eyes and along her arms. "Bring forth your brother."

Fiero turned to his mate, believing that he had heard her whispering some form of prayer but instead finding himself staring at something extraordinary. Ekata was standing where she had been but her hands were now outstretched towards the flames, the silver swirls on her body glistening brightly in the moonlight but the biggest change was her eyes that blazed a stunning white. She stared directly at the funeral pyre and he turned when the heat from the flames suddenly erupted in a dazzling array of white flames almost as if the falling snow had become part of it. The wood beneath crashed into the pit below and instantly the pack was alert, wavering and panicky.

But then from the depths of the flames there arose a wolf of white hot flames, and a burning blue gaze which could only be that of Jared's. The creature stepped towards Ekata, the snow around its paws melting away instantly to reveal the soft spring-green grass and the gentle yellow of buttercups underneath. Ekata smiled towards the creature, her white eyes boring into the all-too familiar blue in an exchange of a silent conversation. The white fire wolf tilted his head back and let forth a howl of joy, youth and exuberance that spread through the hearts of all of those who were grieving. It was Jared's call, the one that he had always used since he was a cub.

"Go now," Ekata said with a smile. "We will wait for you."

A sort of smile crossed the wolf's face and despite being made of flames, the creature nuzzled harmlessly against the Volf before turning to his family and leaping playfully at them. Whether following some form of inner instinct or just the possibility that Jared was indeed back with them now, all of his brothers and sisters changed into their wolf forms and chased off after the white fire wolf with howls of joy and mischief almost as if they were cubs again. Rosario and Stefina stared on confused and bewildered but took off after their children after a quick glance between themselves and Ekata.

The female Volf was still staring in the same direction that she had been looking at before and as soon as the last tuft of grey fur disappeared into the distance, the white disappeared from her eyes and she collapsed to the ground.

Fiero quickly moved, catching her and running his fingers across her skin which was burning hot but in a strangely pleasant way. "He is free," she said, sounding overjoyed. "Fiero... I freed him. I didn't..."

"Ekata?" he asked as the girl suddenly passed out in his arms, finding himself to be extremely confused and lost despite knowing deep down that this was something new. He glanced up at his Uncle Disreli, the only other wolf who had remained when the others took off after the fire wolf. "Do you know what has just happened?"

"Something that should be impossible."

~ ~

Laid out to rest on the bed in Disreli's room, Ekata appeared to be slumbering in the quietness of peace and relaxation. Something which Fiero had never actually witnessed her doing before. Gently he ran his fingers over the edges of her face and allowed a small smile to play across his own. "Even like this you are beautiful, my dearest."

"If I wasn't already fully aware that you had taken her as a mate, Fiero," Disreli said with slow and deliberate words, "I would have more than suspected it by now. I am glad that you were her choice in the end."

"In the end?" Fiero turned back to look at the elder, his fingers not quite leaving the human flesh which was a very good sign in the elder's opinion. It spoke of a deeper connection; one that normally would have to be forged over months of courtship and tribulations. In comparison to some, these two had barely known each other a week and were already so well connected that they appeared to be an old loving couple.

Still he nodded slowly. "Yes, even though I have returned to my family over the last few years, I have kept a careful watch on our mysterious little guest for a long time. Longer than many would have been prepared to admit but I am pleased with this outcome for I believe it may prove to the darkest path that brings us to the point of true light."

"You're speaking in riddles, old man," Fiero said in a friendly but rather warning manner, almost as if he didn't like the idea of what the other was suggesting even though he had no possible way of knowing what it was. Another good sign, clearly the boy's soul was far more ancient than anyone had previously guessed and that was a good thing.

Disreli smiled. "Your father used to say the exact same words when he was your age. I used to spend hours making him go crazy with them but I get the impression that would more than likely just annoy you."

Curiosity caught, the young werewolf turned fully to look at Disreli. It was very rare that anyone spoke of his father, not out of disrespect as he had once foolishly believed but more strangely out of a great deal of respect for the other. He was sometimes told that he was very much like his father, in his mannerisms and things he would say but even Rosario would rarely talk about the other wolf in any great detail, simply saying that he was a man who Fiero should recall only when the time was right to do so. Fiero had accused him of sounding too much like Disreli and had promptly dropped the matter, something which was apparently a very likable if irritating habit, he had gained from his mother.

"What does he have to do with this?" He wanted to know so much more about the mysterious man but felt that there was something just a little more pressing him right now. "With what happened to Ekata?"

The elder sighed, shifting slightly. "He has little to do with this situation per se but he played a more important role in the beginning. Such a long time ago."

Fiero was definitely curious now and leaned forward a little, "What role did he play? Please, Uncle, even if is a minor thing it may help us now. Can't you speak of..." Suddenly the cub paused, turning back to look at his mate who had started to mewl quietly in pain. "Ekata?" Gently, he moved the girl so that she was leaning on his body as her temperature had dropped drastically.

Disreli took the opportunity to quietly flick a small bottle over that was just out of the eye line of the two cubs to his eyes and allowed the small purple dust clouds to drift over to the pair.

Slowly the amber eyes opened and the girl looked up at Fiero with confusion. "Is the blood moon rising?" she whispered before their eyes locked together.

Chapter 12

Blood Moon Rising

Siren watched as her brother paced back and forth in an agitated manner, her eyes glistening slightly as mischief and mayhem rose in her mind. "What troubles you, brother?" she asked, tilting her head to the side childishly.

A snarl was her reward and the elder vampire continued to pace back and forth in the same pattern until the younger finally grew distracted enough to rise and start moving off. "Don't you feel it?" The tone was bitter, confused and mixed with an unconfirmed emotion which was trying desperately to hide itself behind the others.

It was the first time that Siren could clearly remember hearing the other sounding concerned and it worried her far more than anything else about this situation. Slowly she turned to look at her elder brother, noting that there was a change to his stance, instead of standing tall and proud with a cocky air about him, Mephistopheles somehow seemed smaller, more gangly and less – the word escaped her when those light grey eyes landed on her and Siren felt a jolt of shock go through her mind.

However, before the thoughts could connect properly, the other vampire snarled dangerously, "Do you feel the change in the air, Siren?"

The girl pulled herself together. "You mean the atmosphere? Yes, I do feel it. Hence why I am going to hunt."

Mephistopheles stared dumbfounded at the beauty of Siren's voice, how it flowed and moved now instead of sounding like a whiny little child who had to be controlled and shouted at constantly. Standing before him was a vampire lady, not a broken doll whom he could manipulate and it just confirmed his suspicion that something was going on here that was far greater than he could understand. It had to do with that wolf of fire, or maybe that was the trigger or a result of what was going on. Something had shifted, something had changed and some inner instinct was telling him that it should be impossible for this to be happening.

"Are you not scared by it?" Mephistopheles said, seeming to come aware of his own voice for a second, how the pitch had changed and altered, going back to a more bratty tone rather than his cruel schooled elegance.

"No, I am hungry," Siren replied, turning away from her brother. "You are free to join me should you wish though."

For the first time in what felt like forever, the elder vampire didn't want to be on his own. Normally he would crave the silence and the freedom from his mewling and pathetic excuses for siblings but tonight he wanted nothing more than to remain by the other. "I don't know what you could be possibly hunting," he scoffed but followed. "There's only vile werewolves around here."

"There's a town not too far away," Siren replied, moving through the growing darkness like water but never straying too far from her elder brother who was following along behind like some lost puppy. "With plenty of fresh necks ready to be drained."

A smirk crossed Mephistopheles' features; maybe that was what he was missing. He hadn't drunk fresh blood for a long while as he had been so focused on tracking down that obnoxious bastard sister of his. Yes, that was a good enough explanation for him and devouring a few virgins would set him back on the right track. He let Siren lead, since she seemed to be aware of where she was going and pretended that he wasn't disturbed by the fact that she knew and he didn't. The Den's defenses virtually shimmered in the trees, and the elder vampire frowned at them as he passed, noting that they were far more complicated than he had previously thought as well as being highly advanced. This was no ordinary pack defense system, these wards and curses were of a level that he had never personally seen.

All thoughts were driven out of his head about the wards when from in front of him a scream ripped through the night and his head snapped to the side. Siren had entered a patch of open ground and at first glance appeared to have tripped. Normally he would have scoffed at her silly movements and berated her for being stupid. But there was something about that wail which spoke instinctively to him and despite his years of not caring in the slightest for his younger siblings, Mephistopheles found himself running forward to grab the girl and pull her into a hug. She was still screaming as he tried to pull her away, incoherent nonsense spilling out of her mouth as per usual and the elder vampire raised his head up to the sky to see what could have possibly distressed her so.

His eyes widened in shock. "No, no way! This is not possible..." The grey eyes tore away from the horrendous object above him and instead focused on the wailing Siren. "Come on! We have to move. Rise, Siren, you have to walk, now!" Mephistopheles virtually dragged the girl upright and started pulling her away from the monstrosity in the sky. He took note of the shadows, how they were like deep pools of ink which were highlighted by the horrid grungy yellow light that was being cast around, the edges of the trees tinged with red. Only once had he gone through this nightmare and he never wanted to experience it ever again. Running blindly, keeping a firm grip on his sister, the vampire stumbled into yet another clearing but here there was a cave in the forest wall.

However, standing outside was a figure, long black hair flowing freely, shimmering in the strange ethereal light that managed to be cast about on this most dangerous night. The creature's tanned skin seemed to glow from within and intricate swirls of silver glistered like distant stars. Mephistopheles just managed to slam his hand over Siren's mouth to stifle the scream and felt his own heart beat rapidly. Some inner instinct was telling him to run, to get away from this monster but he didn't dare make a move or a sound.

There was a sudden movement and the figure turned, the black of the robe she wore making it appear that she was cloaked in a deeper darkness than surrounded her and blazing orange-red eyes with black slits bore into the elder's. He could feel the deadly power behind that gaze, knew that if she wanted then he would be dead in less than a second. *So this is the real power of the silver,* the rational part of his mind managed to think *no wonder Mother craves it so.*

Taking a step back when Ekata took a step towards them, exposing her glistening white fangs with the clear intention to devour their very souls, Mephistopheles found himself entranced. He suddenly couldn't move, even though he knew that he needed to run and not look back until he was safe. The dark ethereal figure took a few more steps towards him and still he couldn't move. He knew that if he didn't then his death would be swift and unpleasant but there was nothing that allowed him to even break away from that deadly stare.

Suddenly an arrow thunked into the ground in front of the Volf from the side and the creature turned, snarling in the same direction. Mephistopheles didn't need a second invitation, not even bothering to glance back over his shoulder to see who had unwittingly given them the chance to run and escape.

Raphael smirked to himself as he drew forth his own sword. "Always said that you were a coward underneath all of your abilities," he whispered towards the retreating form of the vampire but kept his focus on the creature in front of him. "I won't let you hurt yourself or anyone else tonight, my dearest little sister, at least until Fiero comes and pulls you back from the brink." His own heart was hammering wildly in his chest but he had faced far worse than this situation in the past and wasn't about to be taken down by his beautiful baby sister.

~ ~

Prying open his silver eyes, Fiero was surprised to find himself back in his own bedroom but something didn't feel right. Automatically he twisted his head to the side; instinctively knowing that his mate was not beside him as she ought to be right now but there was something else. Something more pressing that had the guardian worrying. The house was silent, but not of slumber, it was a different kind. As if everyone feared to speak too loud.

The young werewolf frowned, an inner instinct telling him it would be foolhardy to try and break the silence but he also knew that he had to find Ekata before something terrible happened. He rose slowly out of bed, letting his senses roam freely but finding that the world almost seemed to be trapped in some kind of fog that blurred all of his senses to the point where he was just about aware of where he was in the room.

Flicking his ear, he listened deeply trying to focus but found that it was far harder to do than it had ever been before. Almost as if the world was deliberately trying to keep him from something and that thought annoyed him. However, he was aware that something was different with Ekata, she was further away than he had ever expected her to go but she wasn't too far. There was something though, something different about the way she felt. Almost as if something had been released, something that had been trapped for a very long time.

A feeling of dread passed over Fiero and he ran to the window, throwing open the curtains only to reel back at the sight of the full moon. Only this time, instead of being a blazing white, it was blood red. Fiero forced himself to look at it, fighting against every inner instinct that he had to turn tail and hide in the darkest corner until the horrible thing passed and pray that he never come across it ever again. But he knew that this was not the first blood moon he had seen, he knew that he had faced it once before and won out and he wasn't going to be beaten by it this day.

"You won't stop me," he spoke aloud, fingernails extending as he dug into the windowsill to keep himself standing. "I will find her, for better or worse and I will not fear you."

Turning away, he made a grab for his old haversack bag which held a few odds and ends which he always found useful. Throwing a few extra items in without really paying attention to what they were, Fiero willed himself to become a wolf, the change hurting more so than it had done in years but he simply gritted his teeth and made the full transformation. Taking the backpack in his teeth, the large black wolf made strong but slow steps throughout the den, taking note of every last detail and realising that most of his brethren were completely consumed by the raging fear.

Only Disreli remained in any form of coherent sense, sitting on the chair where he had last seen him and the elder turned blazing yellow eyes onto the younger. "Good," the voice was spoken carefully, rough and hewed with the greatest amount of control that could be present right now. "You have awakened when you should have. Go and find her, bring her back and don't give into the temptation that will be given to you."

Fiero nodded, not able to respond with the haversack in his mouth and turned away from the elder werewolf. It took a few good bounds in order for him to get running at any form of speed but seeing that virtually everyone else was

crippled by this whole experience he was secretly amazed
that he was managing this much. He was soon out of the Den
and into the woods, following his homing instincts to locate
his mate and taking little note of the world around him.

Chapter 13

Kiss of Blood

The Blood Moon cast eerie yellow and red light over the landscape, increasing the darkness of the shadows. Fiero couldn't help but feel like he was in some surreal horror movie for a second but caught a whiff of freshly spilt blood and increased his speed. He found himself vaulting over fallen trees, dashing around dark shadows and barreling through twisted ivy vines, which previously had never bothered him. In this strange light however, it felt as though nature was being sucked dry, something was taking the very life force that was given to the planet and corrupting it.

It felt like a force against nature, trying to make everything crumble against a will that was not natural in the slightest and held a disdain for everything that was living of its own free will. This was a trapped monster, something that had been suppressed and denied its right of existence and the werewolf knew that it was trying its very hardest to latch onto his darling mate and make her become its vessel. What was worse was that the monster was probably far closer than it had ever been before but Fiero wasn't about to lose out now. He had just gained what was rightfully his and there was no way that he was going to give it up without a fight.

Charging around a corner, Fiero found himself naturally changing back to his human form, he was near the spring and it shimmered a beautiful shade of innocent white light in the all-consuming darkness. He blinked and stared at the crystal-white water, which shimmered despite his current need to find Ekata and without pausing to think, the werewolf guardian stepped into the water. Tendrils of sparkling silver water rose up, gently caressing his arms, legs and body. For a second he thought that he heard soft words being whispered into his ear but a sudden cold dread passed over him as with a crash, a figure slammed into the ground just short of the waters he was standing in.

The figure rose, standing a little hunched over with his long black hair sticking wildly in a whole host of directions as it had fallen out of the black ribbon it had been tied back with. Pale skin and extended fangs immediately identified that this was a vampire and Fiero moved to grab the other to demand where his mate was but instead found himself pulling the unknown male out of harm's way as a blur of black came at him from the shadows of the forest.

"Ekata!" he yelled, blocking the frenzied female's attack with his own body and pushing her back. "Stop this! It's me, Fiero."

The shadow-thin girl flipped upright, a snarling hiss escaping from the monster with the white fangs whilst the eyes blazed a blood-red with a screamed demand to be satisfied. "Your attempts are pathetic, boy." The voice that spoke wasn't his mate's but Fiero was not about to be put off by such a thing. "I am stronger than that."

"No." Fiero stepped forward, keeping his eyes firmly on the creature and scanning it briefly. "You are not stronger. She is stronger than you will ever be. Release her."

Ekata hissed, animal-like and with a malice that should not exist in the girl ever Fiero thought. "You know nothing, and this girl harbor's a great desire for darkness in her soul. She eagerly gave herself up; she gave in to the vampire."

Shaking his head, Fiero just about kept his anger in check, aware that the figure from before was rising to his feet carefully with weapons prepared. "She doesn't know what it means to be either a vampire or a werewolf! You forced yourself upon her and that is unforgivable."

"She wanted this, she wanted the power and the ability to take on anything that threatened her or her brother," the creature hissed, suddenly charging at Fiero. "That includes you."

Fiero didn't even flinch as the creature's body slammed into him, hissing and clawing and desperately trying to draw blood. The werewolf simply stood his ground, holding the girl out at arm's length and stared levelly at the blazing red eyes. The creature thrashed, slashed and howled at him, determined to get to its goal but the Volf's body was just far too weak to do anything against the almost mature werewolf.

"Ekata," Fiero spoke calmly to the wildly hissing creature being held at arm's length, despite the fact that it continued to slash at him. "Ekata, I know you're there, I know that within the heart of this monster you are there trying to reach out to me. I am here; I am with you... just search for the light. Ekata... my mate, my love... I am here. I am waiting, as I always have been."

The creature continued its movements before it came to an abrupt stop. Fiero stared levelly ahead as he felt a slight shift in the flesh below his fingers. "Fiero?" a voice spoke, almost but not quite Ekata and the girl rose her head, "Fiero... it is me. Come with me to the darkness... come and be with me." The effect would have fooled a lesser man, Fiero reflected as he stared into the wrong-coloured eyes.

Tensing his muscles Fiero gave the creature a hard shake, "Don't try that one with me! That is not my mate. Release her." He shook the creature again, more forcefully this time.

"You'll kill her," the creature hissed, trying to maintain its grip on its current host. "You'll be responsible for her death."

Fiero stopped the shaking. "No. I'll be responsible for giving her life, for giving her a family of her own. I'll be responsible for giving her love and making her never distrust me. I love her more than that to leave her alone in the darkness and even if I ever had to follow her there it would be purely to drag her back to be safely in my arms. Release her and allow her to make her own choice!"

"You cannot deny my existence," the monster screamed as it was shaken again. "She still craves the hot blood of the living!"

"Then she can take mine," Fiero virtually howled towards the creature. "She can take as much as she needs from me because I will never deny her!"

There was a flash across the blood-red eyes, turning them back amber and Fiero pulled the figure into his chest into a sharp hug, placing his lips straight onto hers and feeling the warmth of love and that special bond straight away.

"What if I don't stop?" This time it was Ekata, sounding scared and confused and so unsure but her guardian just smiled in return and ran his large hands through her thick hair.

Gently he shook his head. "Don't you remember, I told you that I would tell you when it was safe to take my blood, my lady."

A look of recognition crossed Ekata's face and slowly she moved towards his neck, her arms wrapping protectively around him. "I remember my knight, if this hurts, then I am sorry from the bottom of my heart."

Fiero tensed as he felt her rough fangs brush his soft skin at his throat for a second before the slightest nip of pain as she punctured the flesh. They remained together, almost as if they were frozen in time and gently the foreboding darkness around them gave away, the shadows retreating rapidly into whatever hell they had come from and the blood moon started to wane, turning to a light pink colour above them.

Feeling her flop in his embrace, Fiero just caught the both of them from falling and stared at her with a smile. Her lips were stained with his blood but the colour had returned to her cheeks and she gently reached for him with her fingers. "Did I hurt you?"

"No, my love," Fiero said, pulling her into a bridal-style hold. "Not even a tiny bit."

Ekata smiled and snuggled her head into his chest, her exhaustion clear to see. Fiero turned to go back to the Den only to find himself face to face with the vampire from before. "Alcarde wants to speak to you both," the vampire said, a smirk of a smile playing on his lips. "I am more than impressed with her choice of mate."

"Who the hell are you?" Fiero challenged, snarling at the vampire out of nothing more than a protective instinct.

"I am Raphael." The vampire bowed courteously towards Fiero. "I am Ekata's elder brother and believe you me, I have been trying to protect her since the day she was born."

Chapter 14

Family Ties

"She needs rest," Fiero said for about the hundredth time in a row. "I know that this Alcarde may want to speak to her but she's exhausted."

Raphael shook his head slowly. "In actuality she's got more strength right now than she ever has in the entire time she has been with you, Fiero." The way he spoke was gentle and firm, not condescending but more like that of a brother who was used to dealing with his younger bratty siblings, it made the werewolf think of Jared just a little too much. "Alcarde would not call the pair of you to his side if he believed that either of you needed rest."

Letting out a sigh, the werewolf glared at the other vampire. "Does it even occur to you that I have no idea who this person is or what he wants with either of us? I just want to take her away from here, we can find some place to be safe and start a family together. Why must we go through all of this?"

"Fiero," Ekata spoke for the first time in a while, still sounding a little on the scared side. "Please don't talk about me as if I'm not right next to you."

Grimacing a little, Fiero sighed and pulled the smaller female closer to himself, feeling relief at being able to do so. "I'm sorry, my love, but I just think the sooner we can get away from here the safer you and for the pack. I do not trust this vampire who has turned up and I have no wish to meet anyone else tonight who could potentially harm you."

Feeling Ekata come to a stop, Fiero took a long look at the female Volf who seemed to have just noticed the presence of the other vampire. She blinked her amber eyes at him in question, frowning. "You are not..."

Raphael had to laugh when the werewolf took up a defensive stance in front of his mate, glowering dangerously at him. He shook his head, raising his hands. "Let her finish before jumping to conclusions, wolf."

Ekata placed a hand on her mate's shoulder before stepping around him to step towards the older vampire, a frown on her features. "You're not like rest of them, are you? You're different... somehow I don't remember you but yet—" Her fingers reached out, touching his skin, which felt so cold and distant yet so warm and familiar.

Before she could utter a syllable, the vampire placed his fingers on her lips. "My name is now Raphael and it will remain so, even if I gain back that which was taken from me. I am sorry I was not able to protect you better but I was lost for a long time."

Fiero blinked. "How can a vampire be lost?"

Raphael smiled sadly, glancing up at the werewolf. "You don't want to know. We must hurry if we are late then Alcarde will not be best pleased."

The black-clad vampire turned and started heading back through the trees. Stepping up behind Ekata, Fiero wrapped his arms protectively around her. "Can we trust him?"

"I would trust him to the ends of the Earth," Ekata replied, "He speaks truthfully even when it would cost him what is most dear to his heart."

"So he is who he claims to be?"

A silent nod was his answer and the girl blinked her strange amber eyes at the disappearing figure. "Yes... but also no. I do not fully know what happened but he is my real brother... the other is related by blood to me but he would never dare to accept me as his equal."

Fiero thought that this all sounded just a little too much on the strange side for him but knew better than to try and argue the point out. Plus, they had to deal with Alcarde which was an option that presented nothing of value to him. Vaguely he had to wonder what made him so uneasy about the name and why he didn't want to meet with the other. He wondered back briefly to his uncle, wondering why he had not spoken to him of his father. He still loved his uncle very much and would seek out his guidance but there was something that just didn't sit right with Fiero. Like someone had told him something a long while ago that he should remember but he could not call it forth no matter how hard he tried.

How was it possible for someone, whether they be a creature of the night world or not, to alter memories but yet have it set on a trigger so that they could come back? Though as he now thought about it, Fiero realized that maybe there were many other things that he had forgotten and that unsettled him a little.

However, he felt Ekata shift slightly next to him, clearly the girl was worried and gently he wrapped his fingers around hers to hold them tightly. "It's okay, I'm just being an overly panicky worry-wort, my love. I'm in no pain."

Ekata smiled gently back at him, nodding. "I know and I'm not scared of that. Fiero, are you sure that your—" her words were cut off as his lips found hers once again, bringing forth a warmth in her chest that almost melted all of the ice within her heart and mind. Gently Ekata wrapped herself closer to her mate, taking strength from his abilities to keep her calm and balanced with one simple movement. Most wouldn't be able to calm her after a feeding. "Sorry for going on," she whispered as their lips finally broke, "but I hurt someone once when I fed from them, I hurt them really badly. I don't want to see you like that ever."

Fiero smirked a little cheekily. "Don't worry, you never will. If it ever came to that, I'm pretty sure I could overpower you."

"Clearly you've never annoyed my sister." Raphael cut into the conversation with a tone of voice that said that he knew exactly what he was doing. "Out of the two of them she is the worst for biting, scratching and hitting."

"Raphael." Ekata coyly grinned back at her elder brother, "I do not know what you are talking about in the slightest."

The elder gave his youngest sister a glare, grinning just a little but suddenly snapping his head to the side at the sound of branches breaking. Immediately the vampire had his sword drawn. "Go. Now. Back to the Den, seek out Alcarde before time runs out."

Sharing a quick glance, both mates silently agreed to run as wolves and took off into the snow. The vampire wasn't surprised that they didn't even pause to say any words to him; they were good cubs with plenty of time to master the skills they had been born with. He was already looking forward to his nieces and nephews from this side of the family. A cruel smirk crossed his features. "Right, my *little* brother, let's see what the blood moon made of you shall we?"

There was a growl of distaste from the shadows and slowly Mephistopheles stepped out into the white snow. He looked, quite frankly, to be far lesser than he had been before, more willowy and stretched out as if someone had strapped him to a rack and kept on pulling. His eyes were wild, ravaged by a desperate need to fulfil something that the younger vampire was not probably aware of and it appeared that he had lost some of his stolen status.

Raphael wanted to tease the other for his appearance, to get back at him for everything that had ever been done but he knew better than to try and play dangerous games. He smirked though, knowing that for a short length of time he would have the upper hand and would at least allow Ekata to reach the Den. "Well, at least I get to see what your true colours are now, Mephistopheles," Raphael taunted the other with a low voice. "Or should I call you Angell and remind you of your place?"

The vampire in front of him hissed, fangs dropping as he charged at the elder with speed that in the past would have sent the elder vampire spiraling to the ground. Raphael nimbly dodged to the side, bringing the flat of the blade squarely across the attacker's stomach and arm in what he knew was a stinging blow.

The younger vampire crashed into the snow, hurriedly pulling himself back onto all fours like some rabid creature and snarled again. "You! You are not supposed to be alive!" Mephistopheles charged at the man, trying to latch onto his skin but frustratingly finding Raphael always just out of reach. "You were nothing more than a mewling wreck when I threw you over that cliff edge!"

For a brief second, Raphael remembered that moment. Felt the cold wind on his body and looking up with terrified eyes towards the triumphant face of his younger brother who had just stolen everything from him. He felt the smack of the salt water as it rose to meet his body and then tried to consume it. It was one of the most frightening experiences of his life. But now as he held the younger vampire at arm's length, within mere inches of taking the revenge that had almost gnawed away at his heart for the past quarter of a century, the elder understood what Alcarde had said to him many a time.

"*Those who seek revenge are usually looking to correct a mistake in their own lives. Your brother, though he did a terrible thing to you, is but a pawn in this grand game of chess and he will fall like all the others. It is up to you if it is by your hand or by another's.*"

"You should have thought to kill me outright when you stole what was mine, Angell," Raphael whispered, his eyes never leaving the raging boy in front of him. "But now I see you, I realise that you are just a child. Abandoned by our mother like the rest of us and desperate to gain what you believe will make her love you."

"Shut up!" Mephistopheles yelled, clawing at the skin on the others arm. "I will finish the job this time and present your head on a platter to her before I rip out her own heart and devour it."

A sudden sting to the side of the face paused the frantic vampire's thoughts and Mephistopheles felt some of the anger suddenly leave him. Had Raphael really just struck him across the face like that? Why did it hurt so much? He hated this vampire in front of him, wanted nothing more than to see him dead and gone... why did a simple slap to the face genuinely hurt?

"Think straight for once in your useless little life," Raphael said. "Many have tried to claim Cresta Du Winter's powers and body since the death of her husband and none have succeeded! You claim that you want to kill her and devour her powers but she is a true elder vampire who will crush you like a pawn."

"No, I am the one in control at that accursed place." Mephistopheles finally found some skin on his brother's arms and tore against it with his claws, Raphael didn't even flinch, "She will merely start the rituals and that I shall steal all of their power! I am the one who she favours."

Raphael shook his head. "Mother favours no one but herself."

With a simple movement, he threw the other vampire back into one of the thickened oak trees. "If you had ever opened your eyes you would have realised that a long time ago. She wants nothing but power and prays on those who want the same, only to manipulate them and bring them to their knees at the opportune moment. The only reason that Siren and Akira aren't targeted is simply because they hide their true selves well, even the twins managed it. You have signed your own death sentence by agreeing to help her... I wish you could see that."

"Don't talk to me as if I am your equal!" Mephistopheles tried to pull himself up but found that his strength was gone for now. "You are dead, nameless and without anything in the world! You are nothing but a ghoul of a vampire, following some petty orders from a bigger monster who you don't even know!"

For a second, the elder vampire was silent, regarding the younger below him. "I am more than you because I have the strength to let you be your own undoing. You may have attempted to take away my world from me but you failed to realize that there are far greater things in the world than a name and a status." His eyes held a sort of pity in them. "My name is Raphael Morgue now and unlike you, I hold a love of a beautiful woman and my own children. I am still an elder brother but I am also a husband and a father. You may have stolen away my name and some of my power but you didn't even touch my life beyond that of a few years making friends with the fish who swam around my watery grave. You are a fool, Angell, a brave one but a fool all the same."

"So, now what?" Angell snarled. "You going to kill me?"

"No, there would be no point because you still have a part to play." Raphael stepped forward, pulling out a dagger. "But I am going to wound you so that when the time is right, you'll have a reminder about our little conversation." With a sharp movement, the dagger was impaled through Mephistopheles' shoulder and into the tree behind him before Raphael raised himself up and disappeared into the darkness of the night. He knew already that the other would regain his senses and would be back to cause uttermost mayhem but maybe now he would start to think like a vampire, rather than some demented little brat who was under the complete control of their sire.

Chapter 15

Parting Kiss

It was Ekata who pulled up short first, causing Fiero to barrel into her which in turn made them barrel down towards the small slope on the furthest side of the den. The two wolves were a tangle of black and white for a few seconds before they were able to pull themselves upright. Fiero glanced at his mate and placed a paw on the ground to step forward but was surprised when he received a nip from the younger female. Gently he turned back around to frown at her. "What's the matter, my love?"

"Don't you feel the difference?" she replied back, aware that they weren't talking in the way that humans would do but the female Volf decided that she would ask about it later.

The dark wolf in front of her blinked before turning back to the Den with a curious gaze. On the surface everything looked exactly the same as it always had done, the ramshackle house which was used to keep most humans from venturing too close was still just about standing even though it looked even more dilapidated than it had previously looked. The snowfall, which had reached the logs and intertwining branches, was still present as were the icicles and there was a sense of calm over the whole place.

Gently, he sniffed the air and stepped back. "They're here, aren't they?"

"One of them is," Ekata replied, moving to stand next to her mate. "The other will probably join as soon as Raphael has dealt with him. If, of course, there was not some form of time alteration."

"Please tell me that neither one of them can do that," Fiero asked, already feeling the headache that was coming on even through his thick fur.

The white wolf shook her head in response. "Your uncle can."

That caused a bristle to go through Fiero; surely Disreli would not dare put them in danger like that. Even if he wanted to test them, hadn't they already been through enough? However, there was a nagging thought in the back of Fiero's head that this situation wasn't as complicated as Ekata was making out. "We may have to risk it, if we are to meet with this Alcarde," he said slowly and sniffed the air deeply. "I do not smell blood or fear, maybe they are resting after that moon?"

"I would think not," Ekata said, but knew to trust her mate's instincts. "But I have been tricked before by such peace."

Licking at the soft velvety ears, Fiero somehow managed to make his wolf-faced features smile towards the other. "I know, but as long as I'm here you have nothing to fear. If this is a trap, I'll bite the head off everyone who tries to hurt you."

The white wolf nodded in response, her amber eyes glimmering brightly and they carefully set off towards the Den together, watching for anything that could be possibly out of place or indicate that something was about to leap out. Fiero kept himself in front, though wished that he somehow could have another following them so that there was something protecting them from the rear as well but he couldn't think of anyone he would trust enough to do such a thing.

The sense of calm continued deep within the Den and it was clear that all of his family were resting after their ordeal. Having been too young to recall the effects of the blood moon, both wolves carefully made their way through the pleasant darkness watching for anything that could expose a trap or another form of danger to them. Ekata stuck close to Fiero, taking comfort in his presence and also finding that she longed to remain closer now than she had ever done. How the male was even still able to walk was a complete mystery to her and she could still smell the ever-so tempting scent of his blood but she knew that she didn't crave it.

Aware that he was growing concerned, she lightly nuzzled against his side and tried to calm her raging heart a little so as to no longer worry him. Though she also got the impression that he would worry about her even when there was nothing for him to worry about.

Before she could muse on this any further however, a new scent caught her attention and for a second a stab of fear went through her heart as she thought of nothing but darkness and a bleak world where no one ever came to seek her and her twin brother. However, the next second, Ekata felt an elation the likes of which she had not felt in such a long time. The scent was suddenly bright and cheerful, bringing forth childish instincts and delight that just wanted to run away with her and for the first time in a long while,

Ekata allowed herself to follow them. She bounded past Fiero with a happy-sounding howl, probably freaking her mate out beyond anything else and hurried to where the scent was.

"Ekata!" Fiero called, feeling his heart beat raise as he raced after the small white female, wondering what had suddenly grabbed her. He too had picked up the scent but had been more confused by it. He felt as though he should recognise it from somewhere but could not place it and after everything that they had gone through he didn't really feel like taking too many risks right now. However, since his mate had gone bounding off towards it, he had no choice but to follow her and hope that whatever was waiting meant no ill harm to the Volf.

So it was a bit of a shock when he rounded a corner to find himself almost snout-to-snout with possibly the largest wolf that he had ever seen in his life. This creature was almost double the size of any that had come before him, he looked even bigger than what he could remember his father looking and his fur was a midnight-black but laced with a shimmering red colour that reminded Fiero of the moon that had been present not an hour ago in the sky. Stunning white eyes glistened out of the fur, almost appearing unreal and blind but Fiero got the distinct impression that the wolf before him was staring directly at him, judging and appraising him even though he really had no right as far as Fiero was concerned.

The younger wolf held the elder's gaze determinedly, still somewhat surprised that the white wolf was snuggling up against this huge monster almost as if it were a long-lost parent but Fiero also knew that the girl was in no immediate danger. "Who are you?" Fiero asked, politely but with just enough warning in his voice to suggest that he was not to be messed with right now, "and what do you want?"

A deep rumbling chuckle that almost made him think back to his cub days came to his ears and the reddish-black wolf visibly relaxed. "So you're her mate and guardian. I knew you were special the first time I clasped eyes on you but I wouldn't have ever figured that we would meet in this way again, Fiero."

Blinking in shock, the werewolf stared down at the other and tilted his head in question. "How do you know my name?"

The elder wolf smiled. "I know a lot about you, Fiero Numéire, from the day you were born to the day that led you to this very meeting with me. I suspected that you would play a grand part in this adventure but I did not guess that you would be so important." He sighed gently. "If I had realised I would have demanded that Rosario bring you to the Hunters Guild to be raised as a Guardian but maybe this way was better for the pair of you. You certainly have captured her heart far greater than I would have suspected."

Fiero frowned. "Wait... you know the Hunters Guild?"

"I made the Hunters Guild boy." The wolf smiled. "I was the first of our kind to try and impose the rules on how everything should be governed with contact with humans."

"Oh." Fiero blinked lazily and then clicked. "Wait, you're Neph—"

There was a snort. "No. That may have been a name once associated with me but it is not mine. My name is Alcarde and I've come to be an aid to you, Fiero."

"An aid to me?" Fiero frowned, looking highly uncomfortable. "Unless you plan on helping me to get my mate out of here I don't see how you can aid me any further tonight."

Slowly the large wolf's head turned to the white wolf that was still happily snuggled against his fur and gently he reached out, licking the top of the creature's head. It was a gentle movement, very much like that of a parent and Fiero found himself only wanting to get closer to share in some of the peace which his mate was currently feeling. Normally other males were regarded as a potential threat unless they were of close relative status but strangely, Fiero felt nothing to make him wary of the big black wolf next to him.

Ekata looked up as he approached, gently licking at his muzzle with a smile and a hum. "He always talks in strange ways like that. Do not fear my love; he is here to help one way or another."

There came another deeper chuckle from the creature, up this close Fiero could smell that he was not entirely wolf but his scent was hard to pinpoint. He smelt of vampire, werewolf, demon, changeling and other creatures the likes of which the young werewolf had never really come into contact with before. "Yes, I am here to help but for now you must rest, young one. Your body and mind will need it and I cannot guarantee how long it will last once the red from the moon fades as that is all which is keeping you standing right now. Rest, the pair of you. I shall keep an eye out for any trouble and will wake you when the time is right."

For a few seconds, Fiero felt like backing away and continuing to find his own safe place for Ekata but a gentle pressure on his mind made him give in and snuggle down next to his mate in the thick warm fur of the larger creature. Within seconds the pair were soundly asleep, Ekata reverting to her human form and subconsciously Fiero shifting back to his own as well. Alcarde watched as the pair automatically gravitated towards one another into a protective embrace and he barely nodded at Rosario when the old-looking wolf came and covered them both together with a blanket.

"It's not fair to do this to them, Alcarde," Rosario whispered to him, his eyes still a little lost from what had gone on before. "Surely you can twist the fates or something?"

The large black wolf shook his head. "No. This time I cannot. Though I dearly wish that I could. They are strong though, stronger than I could have hoped for them to be. This has to happen; else all may be lost."

~ ~ ~

The night gave way to day and the day gave way to night. The moon was full in the sky once again but this time it remained its usual reflective white colour though just faintly there were occasional swirls of silver and gold just visible as they intertwined together. Amber eyes snapped open, whether waking from a dream or else some other inner instinct it was hard to say but Ekata gently rose to a sitting position and glanced around the Den. Everything was covered in silence, clearly the pack recovering from the effects of the blood moon. But there was another scent, a warning sign that made her shiver and want nothing more than to disappear.

However though, her life was different now and she couldn't just up and run whenever she felt their presence. Though she paused, realising that the silence was too deep, the sounds of unnatural slumber replacing those which over the last week she had come to identify with the large pack. Turning to her slumbering mate, Ekata shook him desperately, hoping that he would not be affected by it in the slightest. "Fiero," she whispered, trying not to raise her voice too much as panic gripped at her. "Fiero, wake up. We have to go."

The young werewolf grumbled and twisted over onto his other side with a groan that sounded something akin to, "Just a few more minutes." Then his nose twitched with scents and Fiero sat bolt upright, silver eyes gleaming as clearly he too realised the unnaturalness of the whole situation.

Turning quickly to his mate, he nodded silently at her before raising and helping her up to her feet. There were already packs waiting for them, presumably left by Stefina from the smell and quickly the male pulled a worn but still rather pretty cream dress over his mate's head. "We head south," he whispered, hurriedly and slightly cursing as he struggled to pull on his own clothes. "Head for the township and go from there. They would be crazy to even attempt to follow us that far."

Ekata nodded, finishing tugging the shirt loosely over the broad chest that she knew only too well. They both stopped dead when a low whistle caught their attention; clearly the vampire siblings were close and had worked out where they were. A shiver went through the female Volf and quickly she pulled Fiero's face close to hers, their lips brushing together as they so frequently did but this time it was to give her just a little more courage. "The town to the south of here?"

"Yes," he whispered and grabbed her hand, heading quickly out of the room and only sparing a glance back to the slumbering Alcarde. "There's a small church with an unusual shrine out of the front, if we get separated for any reason make straight for it."

No more words were spoken and the pair made their way quickly out into the snowy weather which seemed to be blowing up a blizzard unlike anything that had been seen in years. Fiero pulled Ekata close, knowing that wolf forms would be far easier but somehow he was reluctant to change. They barely got three hundred yards into the snow before there was a twang of a crossbow bolt and Fiero let out a wail of pain. He tumbled down to the snow below, red blood splattering the frozen ice crystals.

"Ekata, run!" he yelled immediately, shoving the girl forward and away from him. "Don't look back, baby, just run! Run... get to the town. I'll be there; I'll be waiting for you! Run!"

Terror pushed her into the swirling snow, despite every last instinct screaming at her to remain where she was, to stay with her mate but his voice just kept echoing inside her head.

Fiero hissed and ripped the bolt out of his side, cursing at the pain which ran through his body. "Run, Ekata, don't stop running. I will find you again, I promise."

Another pain-filled yell escaped him with a hand latched onto his injury, causing a burning sensation to go through his torso. "You'll never see her again, wolf," Mephistopheles growled dangerously to him. "No matter how connected to her you are."

The grey eyes flared a dangerous blood-red and the next thing Fiero knew, he was tumbling down a dark hill and crashing into a series of fallen branches next to a river which had a fine sheet of ice over the surface. The once brilliant white flowers were now wilting and passing back into the ground below. "Run, Ekata, keep running. Don't stop, run... run." The mantra repeated constantly past his frozen lips, fighting off a wave of sleep which wanted to claim him.

Chapter 16

Full Moon

Mephistopheles easily kept pace with Siren, the girl having recovered from her ordeal and was hell-bent on revenge. It had been easy to get her to be fully back under his control, and Mephistopheles felt a renewed sense of energy fueling his movements.

The blizzard raged angrily around them, nature riling itself up against her will purely for the purpose of separating the mated pair. Whilst the vampire had been stung viciously by a brother he thought long dead to the world, he had come out of the ordeal with fresh ideas and a dangerous temper which needed to be fully sated. He knew that if the werewolf remained by the girl's side then they would stand next to no chance against him.

Whilst he was still only a young cub, there was more strength hidden beyond the outward appearance than even Mephistopheles would have liked to have guessed at. Especially now that something had awoken in him, those silver eyes a deadly indicator that this was not a creature to be messed with. So Siren had called forth her powers, created illusions and dwindling thoughts in the slumbering wolf's mind in an attempt to knock him down a few notches on the mental capacity. As far as either vampire could tell, the plan was working as the wolf had let his mate go, telling her to run and meet at a place where she could not possibly get to.

"She is not far," Siren said her voice level and barely even breaking as she concentrated to keep the raging storm off of them. "Though I can't read her yet."

Mephistopheles grinned. "That doesn't matter. I doubt that you would be able to read her regardless. It's a shame that we just have to capture her, I'm sure that even a single drop of her blood would be enough to grant powers unlike any that we have ever seen."

Siren remained silent, keeping her thoughts to herself. She knew what she had to do, she had always known what she had to do but it was always best to wait for the opportune moment. Plus, this situation was far more complicated as she had to not be caught else her brother would more than likely kill her. Sometimes the young vampire would muse on the question as to why her brother hadn't already killed the rest of his siblings but forced those thoughts out of her mind. She had only one job to do and she would see it through to the end.

They reached what must have been an old dried out landlocked river and stuck directly in the middle was Ekata, the snow storm raging all around her. The winds buffering at her human body, the snow and ice tearing at her skin. She had lost her way, given into the despair which had always been just below the surface and had panicked. Just as Mephistopheles had said she would do.

The male vampire smirked in victory, and glanced towards his sister. "Seal this area and make it so she can't get out."

Siren nodded and extended her hands, creating a barrier around the circumference of the old dried out lake. The winds stopped and Ekata whirled around, her eyes alight with fear but determination rolling off her very soul. "You will not take me," she stated boldly towards the approaching vampire. "Not tonight."

Mephistopheles smirked slightly, assured of his success. "Unlike the times before, freak, you are trapped and there is nothing you can do about it this time. Think that pathetic male is going to come and rescue you? He's dying in the bottom of a ditch, freezing to death like he should have done a long time ago."

A deadly glare was sent his way, the amber eyes blazing with a feral light that reminded him of the creature the girl had briefly become when the blood moon had risen. There was no chance that he would let her awaken that side of her again, especially as he now knew the horrid effects the moon had upon himself. He hated to admit it but he had been driven to the point of madness and terror and had nearly gone over the brink.

Only the absolute certainty that his end was not going to be brought about by such a poor excuse of a sibling had been the thing to keep him on the right track. Well, maybe getting his butt kicked with next to no problems by that other bastard vampire had helped a little too but he wouldn't think of that right now. He nearly had the Silver Maiden in his grasp and he would be one step closer to gaining the power that she held within her.

Still Ekata had not said a word towards him about her mate, her eyes remaining cold and level and her stance suggesting a warrior. It was peculiar, how her moods and attitudes could change so quickly without a pause but the vampire chose to ignore it right now. "Come now, you know you can't win this time. You are sealed in this place and if you try to take me on you know what will happen. For once I'm going to give you a chance to make this easy on yourself. I'll spare the male and the pack that took you in like the fools they are if you just come with me and we'll go and pay mother a visit. How does that sound?"

"Like the tongue of a snake offering forbidden fruit," Ekata said in reply, an edge of fear to her voice which marked her as still being a terrified cub. "I wouldn't trust you to keep even a promise you made to that woman who dares to call herself mother. You will not take me." Carefully she stepped back. "And if you do, it will only lead to your demise in the long run."

Strangely a chuckle, deep and loathsome escaped the vampire and he glanced at the young girl with a surprising glint to his eyes. "That sounded very much like a challenge, little lost Volf, do you really think that you can take me on? Do you really have anything in that small little body of yours that could sway me? I would gladly rip you apart if it meant I could steal that power from you but unfortunately I need you whole in order to do something like that. Now, final chance before I withdraw my offer and send you into the dark abyss of a dreaded slumber. Come with me, willingly and I'll spare the wolf and his family. You have my word."

Before Mephistopheles could even finish the sentence, something struck into him from the side and sent him tumbling into the snow. It snarled briefly, flashes of white teeth and cold black eyes lingering just for a second before searing hot pain shot through his arm and side. With a snarl, he leapt upright and summoned forth a lethal whip of fire which snaked out towards the girl and latched onto her wrist. Ekata merely glanced at it and the fire sizzled out, replaced immediately by ice which cracked and snapped harmlessly as the strange white fire wolf raced into it and then stood protectively in front of Ekata with a snarl.

Siren watched the horror on her brother's face growing and remained impassive as she felt a figure approach her from behind. "I'll drop the barrier for you, but you will have to make it look good for my sake, else he will suspect. "

The figure nodded, stepping closer and not speaking a word, silently watching the pair fight below with his silver eyes burning. "She seems different from before, more driven." His voice just as quiet and level but held a note of age to it.

"Mhm," Siren confirmed with a slight noise. "When you're pregnant, it does that to you, Fiero."

Turning to look at the red-haired vampire who grinned at him and nodded, Fiero turned his attention back to the Volf who was still just standing her ground. "I thought that she would be too young still but life anew is something precious." His steely gaze turned onto the female vampire for a few seconds. "Did you really need to murder my cousin?"

"An unfortunate consequence," Siren said, looking straight ahead. "But one that was fated I am afraid. However, Jared still lives in that form and he will do until the day that she dies. Which I am counting on you to make to be a very long and happy time."

"How far are the others?" Fiero asked, shivering despite himself as he glared at the male vampire who was trying to hurt his mate.

Siren paused. "Alcarde won't approach here for a while. We cannot interfere, you know that. But when you need us, send forth the call and we shall be by your side."

Nodding, Fiero prepared himself for this battle even though he already knew that he would lose it because that was what had to happen. Passively he reached around his neck, feeling for the pendant of white wings and wondered why Disreli had blocked all of his memories of training to be a Hunter but figured that the old wolf was making sure that true emotions won out rather than a basic illusion. He was sure that Rosario was going to have a field day with him when he found out. A final glance was sent towards Siren and there was barely a nod of confirmation between the two of them as Fiero raised his hand high into the air to strike towards the female vampire.

Snarling, Mephistopheles dug into his cloak and pulled forth a long blade that shimmered a deadly-looking red. Dark runes flashed on the surface, molding and changing instinctively and he charged towards the Volf, ducking a pounce from the flame wolf and raising the blade high above his head. He barely had the chance to blink as Ekata merely half-hunkered down at the last second and threw her arm out in front of herself to his stomach and whispered something under her breath.

The vampire found himself flung backwards by a pulse of white light, which escaped from her fingertips. He bit back a furious raging yell and stood up, glaring at her but there was a slight smirk to his features as well. "Hmmm, seems that you have somehow grown just a little bit on the stronger side. Either that or something else has changed within you... little girl..."

There was a second's pause from the female Volf, her attention distracted by the words and clearly taken the moment to study herself and realise just what he could be talking about.

Fiero took it as his cue and slammed suddenly into Siren, using a well-timed flurry of glitter to make it appear that he had struck her with a sunlight spell. The werewolf let out a howl which ripped through the night as the barrier around them shattered and was quick to charge at the Mephistopheles, just stopping him short of hurting the Silver Maiden and sending the vampire reeling back into the snow banks. "I thought you would have learned your lesson by now, bloodsucker, you will not hurt my mate."

Ekata stared in shock towards the werewolf, she knew instinctively that it was her Fiero but he somehow appeared different. A touch older with stronger muscles and a more focused mind. But he was still the playful cub that she had fallen in love with. "Fiero?" she asked as he withdrew a blade, which was long, thin, and the colour of freshly-formed ice. "What happened to you?"

"Later, my love." Fiero shot a beaming and toothy smile towards the girl. "Once we are free of this I shall explain it all to you."

Mephistopheles came charging back at them at that point, slashing down at the werewolf and determined to bring forth his downfall. However, each and every slash towards him was deflected, parried and countered with speed, grace and agility that such a young cub could not possibly hold or hope to convey. Pulling back, the vampire snarled dangerously, fangs dropping to hiss dangerously, "How? How have you changed, you mangled patch of fur? You can't be any different from that sprawling mess I left back there."

"There are things in this world that you don't understand, vampire," Fiero retorted back slowly, never once taking his eyes off the monster in front of him. "Maybe you should have paid more attention to the lessons your father tried to teach you all of those years ago and then you may have a better understanding of everything!"

"How dare you," the tone of voice was low and deadly pitched, the eyes blazing with an anger the likes of which Fiero had only ever seen once before, "even mention that monster!"

Suddenly, the ground below Fiero cracked and crumbled, almost sending him tumbling into the dark abyss of nightmares that appeared below his feet. For a few seconds Fiero fought against it, leaping from rock to fallen tree branch to small floating lump of land, slashing at any of the creatures that loomed up out of the shadows or were simply called into existence by the enraged vampire. He had been warned that Mephistopheles could call forth the inner darkness within him, but he had not expected it to be anything like this.

"Fiero!" Ekata screamed, watching in horror as the nightmare which Mephistopheles called forth attacked her mate as the inner darkness started spreading out in a circle from the enraged vampire. Siren was sent tumbling into the snow-covered ditch by one of the shadowy creatures, blood spurting from a wound, and Ekata could distantly hear the horrified yells of the pack as the darkness seeped out further. The town she had been told to stumble towards would also be affected and the Volf knew that if she didn't stop this there would be innocent blood on her hands.

Jared, in his fire-wolf form, snapped and growled at anything that came anywhere near her and drove them back but she knew that he was tiring. Her eyes rose to the sky, finding the full moon blazing as it reflected the light of the sun on the other side of the planet and she knew what she had to do. Pressing her fingertips lightly to her stomach, she tried to reach out to the tiny little life sources that were just there, a day or two old and steadily growing. "I will protect you, I will save them for you. For you all."

Clapping her hands together in front of her, Ekata concentrated and slowly closed her eyes whilst staring up at the full moon, before whispering "Eros."

Slowly at first but steadily rising, the silver swirls on her body glowed and then seemed to rise out of her skin before piercing forward in a series of deadly long spears of silver light. Some flew towards the creatures of nightmares, freezing them in place or else completely possessing the darkness, changing their colour to a brilliant snow white and making them turn on their previous counterparts to help drive them back to the nightmare that they had originally come from. Two slightly darker spirals made their way over to Fiero and Siren, healing them of their wounds and bringing them back from the point of death.

A few bright flurries shot up into the air like fireworks, dispersing brightly and heading out towards the Den and the town in order to protect it further. The rest strove towards Mephistopheles, breaking his concentration and attacking him in wave after wave of blasts, grabbing vines and the occasional creature which would take a bite out of him or else claw and scratch. Mephistopheles growled in rage as his concentration was broken, the nightmares ending in a splutter and he glared towards his sister. "You... how can you be so powerful when all you are is nothing but a miserable pipsqueak with no one to call your own?"

Suddenly he launched himself at the girl, before either Fiero, Siren or Jared could move to react and grabbed her by the throat, plunging the sword into the stomach, which made the amber eyes flash open, and the power dissipate. "You are nothing but a worthless scum who was granted this power by chance!" he screamed into her face, rage fueling him. "You are worthless and unable to wield such a gift!"

Ekata merely blinked at the man in front of her, showing no signs of sadness or fear. "You are just like her," she said slowly. "You don't see what is in front of you. You are the one who needs pity."

Slowly her eyes closed, her body going limp in his grasp and Mephistopheles stared in complete confusion. The next second there came a glowing golden light from inside the girl's chest and the silver lines on her body glowed brighter than they had ever done before. There was an implosion of blinding silver light and the entire area suddenly flooded until there was nothing left but a stinging whiteness.

Chapter 17

Don't Believe your Eyes

Mephistopheles blinked his grey eyes in confusion and looked down at the girl in his arms. She was knocked out, still and silent but breathing. He noticed that she was once again covered in cuts, mud and bruises and the dress she wore was slightly tattered and faded. But there was a serene smile on her face, one of understanding which confused him. Turning back to the battlefield, he blinked at finding himself near to the edge of the forest, far away from where he had been not moments before and there was a cart approaching him being drawn by Siren who looked just as crazy as she always looked. Slowly, he blinked, looking around for any signs of the guardian or the other wolves and just faintly smelt the effects of a sleeping spell.

That was right, they had cast a deep slumber spell on the Den of the pack that had taken the girl in not a few nights ago so that it would be easier to just slip into the place and capture the girl unawares. Presumably Siren must have played around with a few of the spell ingredients and brought about some form of living dream upon them as well. Though Mephistopheles did have to briefly wonder why he was affected by such things. Unless the skitzy girl that was his sister had gone a little too mad with the sprinkling of the powder and caused some to land in his eyes which was perfectly possible.

Shaking his head, he scooped the disgusting Volf up into his arms and made towards the cart, smirking towards his sister who had clearly gotten the girl a coffin to ride in which was ironic given what she was. Laying her down, he stared at her with the strangest sense of confusion, watching as her hands almost instinctively went to her stomach to rest gently on top of it but shook his head and slammed the lid shut, ensuring that the lock was tight and strong.

"What did you put in that sleeping spell?" he asked towards the red-haired vampire who gave him a bewildered look before shrugging and rushing off to play with one of the followers who had caught her fancy.

Mephistopheles signaled to the driver to start them moving and made his way down to the ground, watching as a few other carts made their way along the track. A raven cawed at him as it came into land on his arm, a fresh catch in its mouth and a note attached to its leg. Reading the message, he scratched a reply before sending the creature on with a shake of his head. "Time is unimportant, mother."

He sighed, long and hard before turning and setting off, casually clambering onto one of the last carts. For a second he felt like someone was watching him but dismissed the feeling and lay down to rest in his luxurious covered bed. As far as he was concerned he had worked extraordinarily hard the last few months and a rest was just what he needed.

Watching from higher up the valley, a young man appearing to be in his early twenties glanced down at the small white pocket watch which glimmered with golden and silver swirls before gently closing it with a slight click and handing it across to a spirit with black hair and blazing blue eyes. "You best hurry back to Dymas, we're getting close."

The spirit nodded. "Yeah. Though how he does this I really don't want to know."

The vampire nodded. "Too true you don't."

"What about him?" The spirit indicated the slumbering werewolf on the floor next to Alcarde's feet as he quickly put away the pocket watch in the depths of his coat pockets.

Looking down at Fiero, the young man, named Belial, smiled faintly. "He'll be asleep as long as she is. They are connected almost perfectly. Their power is immense and so dangerous in the singular context."

"Hence why there always has to be another to balance." Tyra sighed, but smiled proudly. "I look forward to meeting you again, even if my memory may be a little hazy."

Belial nodded and let the spirit go, to return to her own charge and to a time before all of this. His light-grey eyes wandered back to the retreating carts, noting where Alcarde was and wondering if the man ever considered the consequences of his actions before doing them. However, a smirk crossed his features, somehow he felt that if his father had ever done such a thing then even he wouldn't have been born into the world.

Poem Translation
"By river and by stars,
We shall find one another
My hope, my love,
Forever eternal,
Blooming forth from first spring sun
To warm the heart
Seal the fate
Bring us back together
Peace and harmony
Will be ours to make or break
But by your side I will stand
Forever eternal
You are my lady
Nothing can change that
I wait for you to come back
So that the world can be
As it should be"